To / 1

CW00621224

The Rise and Fall
of a
Salesman Entrepreneur

Hope you enjoy :)

The Rise and Fall
of a
Salesman Entrepreneur

PAUL FLETCHER

THE CHOIR PRESS

First published in the United Kingdom in 2017 by
The Choir Press

ISBN 978-1-911589-18-1

To Anne, who inspired when giving up
could have been an option.

CHAPTER 1

As I walked into another job interview, I wasn't to know the thirty-seventh prospective job in the nine years since I'd left school would change my life. It started like any other day. I wore my only decent Harvey Willis suit and old tie. It was a hot July day and I climbed up the stairs to the MD's office.

I had never expected to have this opportunity. Two weeks earlier, I had been walking in town and Tommy Harris had come bounding over with a broad grin on his face.

'That job at Spearlings, it's mine!' he exclaimed.

This explained everything. I had wondered why, after applying for a vacancy in the local *Echo*, I'd heard nothing from the largest independent garage in the South West. My heart sank, but when a manila envelope dropped on the mat inviting my presence with Mr Laidlaw of Spearlings I began to believe ...

'Start Monday 3rd. You can sit next to Tommy and collect your green Fiesta Pop on the next Saturday.'

Not a good start. Handing in my notice to Mike, the owner of the petrol station, was made doubly difficult as the night before I'd used the company van. It was teeming down when I stopped at the lights towards the end of the dual carriageway. I looked in my rear view mirror and just knew that the clown in the XR3i was far too close. The screech and thud and neck ache were nothing to the mangled mess that was once the rear of the van. At least he had his insurance details.

I don't know if Mike was more upset with my resignation or the state of the van, but I knew it was best just to leave and not be upset if the Amulet Petrol Station Employee of the Month was now out of reach. Oh well!

*

'Sit next to Tommy and share a desk next to the Victorian heating boiler. Here's your Glass's Guide and order pad. Just bring the deals in when they're done!'

I looked around at the sales team.

Tony 'Fruit' Thomas, the basking shark of a finance manager, like a pantomime villain, all smiles and cheap nylon suit waiting to lock you into a long, expensive finance agreement.

Alan Rooney, every other word a swear word pitched loudly for maximum effect; this big Scotsman liked the sound of his own voice.

Seth Armstrong – a smiling tiger. 'Can I help you at all?' boomed as if by tannoy to any visitors to the showroom. A big cheesy grin followed and usually a derogatory remark, 'timewasters, peasants' being amongst the more innocent ones.

Robbie Stevens, with an ability to be likeable but so many mistakes. Robbie had a beautiful mane of coiffed and highlighted hair; there wasn't a mirror he hadn't looked in or an hour that went by when he wasn't combing his locks. 'Robbie, you don't look well!' was a cruel remark which would send him upstairs to administration in search of a sympathetic office girl.

Jeff Bassett was a cynical older guy who found fault with every customer and colleague. Snide remarks and barbed comments were his speciality and everyone seemed wary of him.

Max Williams was a loud, jolly Welshman who seemed to have the run of the customers. He dealt with everyone who entered the building, most asking, 'Where's Max?' Some of his deals were crazy in that they made little profit, and promises of a free 'Williams pack' exasperated the management, who did little to stop his benevolence. When he was questioned, a wide range of excuses and childlike reasons would make the questioner feel they were wrong. He got away with it again.

Spearlings boasted two senior managers: Clive Laidlaw, a kindly old school headmaster type, and Andre Quisling, who doubled as sales manager and senior salesman. Andre was a yesman, arselicker or brown nose depending on which salesman was aggrieved that day.

'Andre's just here to cherry-pick the best enquiries and flash those "smiling tiger" teeth of his,' growled Max. 'The only person you need to bother with is Clive.'

The overall atmosphere was one of resigned cynicism from the older guys. There were three lads under thirty. Robbie wouldn't notice an atmosphere if it were Chernobyl, Tommy was ingratiating himself with Andre and I wondered, *What have I done?*

After a week of cold shoulders, arctic stares and deafening silence to my cheery 'Good morning's, I went home one night to Susan and declared, 'That's it, I'm going back to Mike for my old job.' Common sense prevailed when Sue pointed out the circumstances of my departure and pride was swallowed.

CHAPTER 2

It's amazing how an innocent crumb of kindness and life can change things. One evening, as I was passing Robbie's desk, he casually announced that he was off to Majorca in the morning for a fortnight's holiday.

'You can have my desk if you like,' he said.

The older guys still regarded the newcomer with total apathy, but I didn't care. I now had my own desk, and customers didn't know office politics or pecking orders. So hard work and obliging people soon raised me from the bottom of the sales board.

Andre was supposed to hold a daily morning meeting, whereby sales business and new stock arrivals were discussed. However, if Clive wasn't watching Andre just didn't bother. His office was an untidy shoe cupboard. Over his head was an electronic flytrap and, as Andre droned on during the rare occasions on which he wished to impress Clive, the only entertainment was watching or hearing a fat bluebottle being zapped in the purple centre that had mesmerised it to its fate.

'Just wait until Saturday when we've finished,' said Charlie. 'You'll be invited into the inner sanctum!'

Charlie was our pitchboy. About eighteen years old and very spotty, this adolescent had plenty of confidence. His role in life was to price up the stock vehicles, park them in their rows on the forecourt and keep all the showroom cars clean and well presented.

'What are you talking about, "inner sanctum"?' I enquired.

'You'll find out! Put it this way: when I came for the interview a year ago Mr Laidlaw asked about O-levels. I told him I didn't take O-levels, just CSEs. Ah well, I'm more interested in spirit levels anyway! You'll find out on Saturday!' He grinned. 'Oh, by the way, when you take in a part-exchange, tag it up and give me the keys!'

'Okay, I ...'

'Tell me whether it's trade or retail and where you've put it. It's just that certain salesmen seem to have their own stock I know nothing about!'

I was sure there was a hidden message in all of that, and that because Charlie and I didn't yet know each other he was verbally testing me for a reaction. It seemed safest not to reply.

'I hate that Bassett – sarky git!' said Charlie.

'What do you mean?' I asked.

'I've just caught him rifling through one of his part-exchanges he put on the top car park behind where the valeters work. It's out of sight, so I don't know it's there. Do you know he looks under the back seat squab for coins before the valeters can claim them? He pinches the radio-cassettes and mats and sells them at car boot sales!'

I didn't believe this until I thought that this was the guy who drank percolated coffee that was at least six hours old and treacle-like, to save paying twenty pence for a vending coffee. He had also polished off six doughnuts brought by a mechanic on his birthday, which were left over and designated for the office girls. What a scrooge!

*

'FRIDAY, SATURDAY. £1,000 off anything on wheels, SALE,' shouted the banners. The local radio station Stour Sound announced this advert every few minutes. The local rag, the *Bradeley Echo*, was full of Spearlings ads announcing the £1,000 minimum part-exchange on all stock vehicles.

'Right, lads, you all know the drill,' announced Andre. 'Take your rows and price 'em all up a grand.'

'What's going on?' I asked after the briefest of meetings.

'I'll tell you what's fucking going on,' boomed Alan. ''Tis our fucking chance to earn some beer money.'

'What does he mean?' I asked Max later.

'Well, let's put it this way,' he said. 'Clive's not that interested in scrap part-exchanges; some are worth a few hundred quid, so obviously they don't come in, do they?' He winked as he said it.

'But Clive will wonder why we've given £1,000 off with no vehicle to show.'

'Hang on,' said Max, 'we're all going to put them up £1,000, so Clive's not bothered. It's just one less banger he's got to dispose of.'

I was beginning to realise that Spearlings was a close den of iniquity. No wonder the older salesmen were wary of newcomers. Problem was, if you didn't join their scams, you would become very unpopular and isolated. This would take careful consideration.

Over the next few weeks I became friendly with Max.

We shared a similar sense of humour and laid-back approach to life. Gentle probing answered all my suspicions that everyone was on a fiddle and Clive and Andre not only knew about the scams, but were involved as well. Although Max wasn't greedy, he admitted the extra 'beer money' came in handy. I'd skirted around all the shenanigans, but I was going to have to either join in or become very isolated.

'Pick me up from home, will you?' asked Max. 'I've got a foreigner to drop off.'

'Sure, I'll follow you,' I replied.

Max lived in very fashionable Prestbury, a suburb of Bradeley. On the way back he was dismissive of my concerns.

'Look, I've worked for Spearlings for fifteen years, from being a family company to being owned by the finance house it is today. It's been the same from day one. Everyone has a little tickle. We're making good money for the company and everyone's happy. Clive's been here for nearly forty years. He knows how to keep the board sweet. What's the problem? If you don't want to join in, Mark, just turn a blind eye and live and let live.'

That's what I decided to do.

*

That Saleday Saturday was the busiest I'd ever seen. Every salesman and even Charlie went non-stop from about 11am onwards. Bargain hunters and whole families descended on Spearlings, enticed by radio and paper adverts. By mid-afternoon there were cars and trade plates up and down the A40 test drive route. Some were accompanied by salesmen, some were on their own. Cars ran out of petrol, queues were outside the finance manager Tony's door. It was manic, but the adrenaline was pumping and it was *fun*.

Eventually by 6.30pm the last customer was leaving. He happened to be my Allegro man and had spent the last ten minutes looking around from my desk and asking, 'What's all the racket from that office?' Hmm. I was about to find out.

When I opened the door it was like New Year's Eve in a Scots pub. The smoke made your eyes sting. Bodies were everywhere and faces were ruddy and ties were dishevelled.

'Get him a drink,' shouted Clive. 'What's your score, Mark?'

'Er, five, I think,' I replied.

'Twenty-eight, then,' said Seth.

'Told you we'd hit thirty this weekend,' said Max.

'How do you work that out?' asked Jeff.

'Well,' – Max had the whole room's attention – 'Alan's always got two for Monday!'

The whole room erupted in a cacophony of laughter. It might have been a mystery to me, but there was no doubt from Alan's shifty look that exaggeration and swearing played a large part in his personality.

For the next half-hour Max held court, telling his Welsh stories and jokes. 'Nothing queer about Carruthers' brought the house down. One by one, as the cans of lager and bottles of scotch were dumped in Clive's waste bin, the lads sloped off.

'Coming up the pub, Mark?' asked Tony. 'It's the tradition!'

'Not tonight. I've got to be in Marlow-on-Stour with Sue; it's booked!'

'I know. Women, eh? Don't forget next Saturday, though; it's part of the Team Spirits that Clive's very keen on.'

Wow, now I could see what Charlie meant by 'spirit levels'.

Sue wasn't so understanding when I crossed the threshold. 'What time do you think this is?'

'It's about eight, but I'll get a new battery for that watch of yours if it's slow.'

'Don't get funny, Mark, we were supposed to be at Mum's for tea at seven. I've told her we'll be late.'

Blimey, this was going to be tough, but I knew I had to keep all the balls in the air. Jobs like this didn't come around that often, and it was either going to end in tears or be the best rollercoaster money could buy. One thing was sure: I wanted to be there for the whole ride.

*

I'd noticed a little weasel-faced scruffy guy in Clive's drinking den on Saturday. His darting dark brown eyes missed nothing.

'Who was that guy with Clive?' I asked Jeff on Monday morning.

'That's Andy Beale. He's a trader, tight as a drum – a nasty piece of work, don't cross him!' he replied.

'Only he's come up to me a couple of times and stuttered, "Got any?" then made a funny sign with his thumb and fingers.'

'What did you say to him?' asked Jeff.

'I didn't,' I replied. 'I thought he was a halfwit.'

That clearly tickled Jeff, who went off chuckling in search of someone. An hour later Max sidled up to me, grinning, and said, 'I hear Andy Beale's been asking you about tax discs.'

'Huh?' I replied, to which he explained that it was common amongst car traders to buy the tax discs of part-exchanges from the salesmen for a percentage of their refundable face value. Andy Beale and Chance Loveday paid the most, but Andy was always on site and bought the most cars. If you wanted to deal with Chance you had to go to his house, and he lived in a remote place by the River Stour off the A40.

'But I thought all the tax discs taken with the part-exchange went to the garage,' I said.

'Well, obviously some do,' said Max, 'but they don't pay you for them, so it's a bit more for the holiday fund. Anyway, everyone's in on it, including Clive, so if you don't play ball you'll spoil it for everyone!'

Oh dear, this was getting serious.

My solution was to give the customer back their tax disc. I told them to get a refund form from the post office and send it off. Unbelievably, some didn't wish to bother and some just looked as if they didn't understand my simple instructions.

As the weeks passed a pattern of life emerged. With enthusiasm and a wide grin, coupled with lots of hard work and patience, this job was like that of an Egon Ronay restaurant critic. Money for old rope.

Mr and Mrs Hobbs were hard work one Monday, coupled with the previous visit last Thursday. They were 'muffies' – a derogatory term aimed at people from a very rural area the other side of the Stour, known as Muffleyford. They were insular and very mistrusting of anyone from the 'big town', Bradeley. They had concentrated on an ex-rental yellow Cavalier, which Clive was extremely keen to sell. It had been in stock from the last 'buyback' deal eighty-six days previously. So, although any deal would be very thin, profit-wise, I was on a minimum commission and with 'extras' it was worth my while to persevere.

Several hours and two more test drives later, a free two-year warranty (worth £295), a free roadfund licence, a free Maxpack (mats and mudflaps) and the deal was struck.

'Fair play to you,' said Jeff. 'I tried to deal with them last year; bloody muffies want everything for nothing.' As he looked at the order he whistled out. 'Looks like he got it; you've outMaxed Max. It's a wonder you didn't agree to fill his tank.'

Little did he know I had!

'Well done, Mark! That Cavalier was going to appear on the Ordnance Survey map, it had grown roots, top of the list. I'll pay you a special,' said Clive.

I felt very pleased when I'd got Clive to sign off a £75 special, together with a £25 commission for the warranty I sold him! The deal was worth £100 to me. Ironic, really, when on paper we sold it to lose £466. Still, on with the next one; it'll all come out in the wash, as Max would say.

I'd arranged delivery for the following weekend, after the road tax and reclean could be enacted. On Saturday I collected the Cavalier from the valeting bay and filled it with petrol at the pumps. Seth was filling an old Capri and looked sheepish. 'The wife's,' he said, as if that excused his obvious fiddling.

I checked the car, put the tax disc in the window and

waited for ten o'clock to arrive. At quarter past I returned to my desk. Tony and Andre were trying to calm Mrs Hobbs down.

'Whatever's wrong?' I enquired.

'What's wrong? I'll tell you what's wrong,' replied Mrs Hobbs. 'I'm not taking that death car home. Look at the number plate, it's JUD!'

The number plate read B166 JUD. 'Jud', as Seth pointed out later, was muffie dialect for 'dead', and they, being superstitious muffie country folk, couldn't imagine a greater curse.

'Come on, George, we're off. We won't be coming here again!'

They stormed off. The deal was dead. The car went back up for sale, but not until I'd driven it nearly empty of fuel. I made a mental note: *Be wary of superstitious muffies.*

Max was in a fine mood, and when I recounted the story he roared.

'That reminds me of when we worked in Muffleyford years ago as managers of a residential care home. Thick as pigshit, some of them. Me and the wife wanted a day off one quiet Thursday, so we asked Albert if he would let out the dogs as we would be late back. I left his instructions, got into the minibus and went to Wales to visit my mum. We rolled back at six-ish with no sign of Albert and the dogs. Seven o'clock came, eight o'clock came. It was nearly nine when three figures emerged from the gloom. "Where the heck have you been, Albert?" "It's your fault, Max," he said, agitated. "What you wrote, you said to come back from the dog walk ASAP after tea. Well, it took 'em until now." "Took what

until now?" I asked. "To have a shit and a piss, like!"
The penny dropped. "*ASAP* means *as soon as possible*,
Albert, not *a shit and a piss*." "Ooh," said Albert – "then
why didn't you say?"'

*

George's office was a tiny room next to Tony on the
right of the showroom. They couldn't be more different.
Tony was meticulous with his empty desk, paper
stacked neatly in trays, chairs at ninety degrees and
phone wire unlooped with the handset in its perfect
cradle. George, however, had paper everywhere, his
desktop covered with ashtrays full of stale, stinking
butts, the room littered with batteries, tyres, bits of
steering columns, headlights, headboards and signs.
You had to kick your way into his office.

George Ferguson was the aftercare manager – the one
the salesmen passed all the mechanical problems to.
'Just ring George, he'll sort it,' was the familiar cry, with
'bloody screamers' from the old guard: the usual
mutterings.

'What's a screamer?' I asked Tommy innocently.

'Oh, that's the term for anyone complaining about
petty faults on a second-hand car – you know, when the
engine's knocking or gearbox crunches, that sort of
thing.'

I must have looked bemused because Tommy added,
'Only kidding, Mark, but seriously, don't get involved.
They'll ask for you and try to get you to fix their car.
Don't!' He startled me. 'Because it's time-consuming,
just act dumb and pass it straight on to George.'

'What if it's the weekend or George is away?'

'Then implement plan B, which involves escaping

through the back of the workshop to disappear for half an hour in your car. Go home or go to the pub, but don't get involved!' Tommy ordered.

This all seemed a little extreme to me.

The first time a lady appeared at my desk saying she had a few problems with her car, I looked over to George's office. I realised he'd gone to lunch five minutes before.

'Let's have a look at your list.'

It had ten different items, ranging from a clunky noise from the passenger door to a strange smell in the boot when it rained.

'I want them fixing now and I want a courtesy car. I've driven twenty miles in my lunch hour and I need to get back now.'

Oh, how reasonable some customers can be!

'Who did you book this in with?' I said.

Blank stare.

'How do you expect me to sort this without any prior warning?'

Blank stare.

She gave me the look that said all salesmen are slippery, slimy snakes that will say anything to sell you something – but when there's a problem . .

'I'll try and get a mechanic to have a look, but it's lunch time and I don't have a loan car. Sorry, but you needed to book . . .'

With that came the Victoria Falls of tears and an embarrassing scene in the showroom that even got Seth and Jeff to look up. Flummoxed, I asked Jeff for advice.

'Tell her to fuck off.'

Not very helpful. Seth was slightly more

accommodating: 'Get rid of her, give her her old car back, or if that's gone find the crappiest part-ex and send her on her way!'

I did as I was told, found her an old Lada without power steering.

'Hope it's got plenty of petrol. Mine's nearly full.'

'Yes, yes – I'll phone you when it's done.'

'Told you,' said Tommy, not too subtly. 'It doesn't pay to be too nice to them. Tell 'em to—'

Yeah, okay, Tommy, I'd got the message, but I knew I couldn't treat people like that.

George returned and quickly struck seven off the list. 'Wear and tear, five-year-old car, what's she expect?' he mumbled under his breath. The remaining three items were fixed by Jim, our mechanic, and some lavender water was sprayed in the boot.

Mrs Stevens returned with her two-year-old three days later. 'It had better be all done!'

'See George over in his office,' I said, pointing.

'Oh, that heap you gave me, I've got weightlifter's arms.'

'See George.'

With that she wandered over, dragging her snotty kid, who started crying, wailing and then screaming. I looked at Tommy, he looked at me and we both burst out laughing.

Slowly, over the next three months, the sales team settled into a routine. As long as the showroom was manned and phones were answered, life was fine – one found a level. High fliers worked hard, lazy salesmen took two-hour lunch breaks. I'd jumped into my own desk, next to Robbie and behind Jeff. Seth, Alan and

Max were as thick as thieves. They spent the quiet times putting the world to rights, smoking and cracking jokes, and they never seemed to see Tommy or me sneak out of the side door.

Of course, with quiet resolve, hard work and determination, the youngsters became the driving force of the sales team. The older guys were happy with their lot; camaraderie, beer tokens and dubious deals seemed to satisfy their daily ambitions.

'Tiddlywinks alright, get a woman if you can, if you can't get a woman get a clean old man!' sang Robbie. This seemed to be his signature tune, which he rendered at least six times daily when the showroom was empty of customers. 'Come with me, Mark; we've got a couple of "stunt cars" to park round the back to wait for the scrappie wagon.'

The scrappie wagon was from Philpott's, the local scrap yard. He collected cars that even the scruffiest of the motor traders deemed sub-standard. Before they were collected, Robbie loved to play his own version of bumper cars. No sooner had I driven the Nissan Cherry ten yards than, *crunch*, a fierce whack hit the rear end. A brown Maxi had been the culprit with a grinning Robbie behind the wheel. Ten minutes later there was not a panel on either car which hadn't taken a hit. Valeters came out of their sheds, and office girls all appeared curious about the commotion.

'Wow, that's what I call fun,' I said.

'Yeah, it certainly relieves any stress and it's the most fun you can have with your clothes on,' said Robbie.

Robbie was not a very prolific car salesman. He was usually in the bottom three on the chart in Andre's office. Behind Andre's desk was a giant board which depicted all the sales of cars, warranties and extras for every salesman in the showroom. Max and I were always the frontrunners followed by Tommy and the others, but Jeff and Robbie were always in the bottom zone. When you went into Andre's office, it was a reminder of why you were there and, for the more competitive, a sense of pride or shame.

However poor Robbie was at selling cars, he more than made up for it in selling himself – especially to the fairer sex. He only ever seemed to have single women for customers. Sitting next to Robbie I heard all his chat-up lines and innuendos, and of course a car handover always ended with 'If you need a service, just give me a ring – oh, and if the car needs one too!' It may have been corny, but many a time I answered his phone to be greeted with 'Robbie, about that service?'

Robbie got into many scrapes. He had a fine young lady at home with a young son called Harry. We all tried to convince him that he was playing with fire, but the thrill of the chase was just too much. It wasn't as if he just went for attractive young ladies. 'Anything in a skirt – in fact, anything with a pulse!' was one of Max's expressions for Robbie.

Slowly over the following months I was persuaded by all the lads to pop into 'the Railway' after work on the Saturday night. This was a newly built theme pub near an industrial estate and was close to my home. On Saturday nights it was the local motor traders' haunt. Jameson's the Vauxhall agent and Grimley's Rover were just two of the local dealers who brought all their sales staff. The atmosphere was terrific and plenty of banter ensued. Friendships and acquaintances were built which lasted for years.

The trick was not to stay for too long or to accept any drinks. It seemed a pity sometimes to sneak away, but if you didn't you would turn into a Jeff or Alan. That pair ended up 'spoofing' for rounds and still being in the pub at closing time. A taxi home and a weekend of silence from their wives; we heard about their problems every Monday morning.

Monday evenings in the Railway were different. Monday was my late night. Once a week you were required to work until 7pm in the summer months. Business was usually slow after 6.30pm, so I'd look up and sneak away for a 'quick one', see some of the rival lads from Jameson's and slip off home. One Monday, when I entered the car park, I noticed Robbie's GTi.

'What are you doing in here?' I called over to Robbie.

'She's kicked me out!' he said. He was dishevelled; he looked awful. 'Can I stay on your sofa, mate?'

'Whoa – what's happened?'

I proceeded to buy Robbie a drink, sat him down and listened to his story.

'Found a pair of panties in my golf bag, she did.'

He failed to explain which particular conquest this was and over the next half-hour he eventually confessed that Marie, his girlfriend, had caught him on seven occasions with different phone numbers, love bites or phone calls to the house. He'd managed to persuade her before that they were not serious, or were just some girl who had become obsessed. However, this time it was different; she'd found these pants stuffed at the bottom of his golf bag and had gone ballistic.

'But Mark, they weren't from any bird I'd been with. I'd just used them to clean my golf balls!'

I gave him a sideways glance 'Yeah, pull the other.'

I took Robbie back to the bar, we had another drink and I chatted with two of the lads from Jameson's while Robbie went to the loo. When he came back he seemed highly agitated.

'My car keys – they've gone!' he shouted. 'I put them on the bar just a minute ago.'

A search ensued; the bar staff didn't have them. We searched his coat and trousers: nothing. The atmosphere in the pub turned very tense.

'I'm going to phone the police,' Robbie said, loudly enough for all the pub to hear. 'The car's disappeared now!'

'Don't do that!' a squeaky female voice cried out. It was one of the Jameson's sales team, a new recruit called Louise. 'I didn't mean any harm – I did it as a bet from all the lads in sales – I just moved it round the corner ...'

'You stupid cow,' said an angry Robbie, 'all my kit's in that car – where is it?'

Robbie and I walked fifty yards round the corner with the keys. All over the back seat of the car were clothes, shoes and so on. The boot was packed with suitcases, a television and a microwave. It seemed very sad; Robbie's whole world was in that car, and for a horrible minute it had seemed even that had been stolen. And no, I didn't put him up on my sofa. I lent him £20 for a bed-and-breakfast. Sue and I had only been married for less than a year and although I trusted her implicitly, Robbie was in a different world.

Days later Robbie's ex and baby left his bungalow in Shotton and moved in with her parents. They wanted nothing from him. Less than two weeks later Robbie had installed Lauren – his long-admiring admin girl from upstairs – in the bungalow.

'Someone's got to iron my shirts and cook my tea,' was his explanation.

*

Trips to the office and administration were kept to a minimum. We took cash, cheques, deposits and balances to the cashiers. If you needed a car taxing urgently you could sometimes bypass the system. Otherwise Harriet, our sales admin lady, would sort out most problems. Harriet was Clive's assistant, nursemaid, barmaid and general dogsbody. She worshipped Clive and dutifully echoed his opinions and prejudices.

'Keep those accountants out of sales,' Clive said on an almost daily basis.

When Ramiz the accountant came into sales, Clive playfully reminded him of his place. 'Does Steve know you're in God's country, Ramiz?'

Steve was Steven Limbrett, the company secretary and Ramiz's boss.

'What's up, the petty cash not balance?' Clive asked cheekily.

Although it was banter, there was an irritability about Clive around accountants. 'Bloody bean counters,' he used to say when the sales lads had their sessions, whether business or a drinking wind-down. 'Don't let them dictate to sales with their percentage mark-ups, days in stock and maximised efficiency.

People buy from people. Trying to complicate sales will kill the golden goose.'

'Don't start him off,' said Seth. 'You know it's coming, Clive. All business are run by accountants now, never mind what the customers want – satisfy the shareholders!'

I left them to their arguments – there were punters on the forecourt.

CHAPTER 3

'You bin into work today, boyo?'

'Er, yes,' I said, not quite recognising the tone on the other end of the line.

'It's Max, yer? Listen, I've just heard something very serious, so get your story right!'

Max proceeded to explain that he had just been tipped off by Chance Loveday that Steve Limbrett had done an investigation into tax disc fraud at Spearlings. Apparently his opposite number at Jameson's had listened to some gossip from Andy Beale's rival car traders, saying it was common knowledge in the trade that Andy had all the salesmen from Spearlings in his pocket. Limbrett had checked all the orders going back a year, written to DVLA at Swansea and found the majority of the tax discs had been cashed in by Andy Beale's AB Autos. Obviously Clive tried to explain that they were part-exchanges Andy had bought, but most of the discs were for cars that Spearlings had subsequently retailed. Andy Beale was summoned in to be interviewed by Steve Limbrett. At first he denied everything but subsequently, after being threatened with the police fraud squad, he sang like a bird. Max went on to say that anyone who sold the discs to

Chance Loveday like he and Andre did were in the clear.

'If you dealt with Andy, Mark, get your story straight,' Max advised.

Although my conscience was clear I still felt sick. All my colleagues were in hot water and I may have been dragged in too.

The atmosphere at Spearlings that Monday morning was one of doom. The bantering and bravado were replaced by long faces and shuffling salesmen. The devil-may-care attitude was replaced with a dawning realisation that cheating and stealing were endemic. By his nature Steve Limbrett hated what he had discovered. It opposed all his training and principles.

We were all summoned into a sales meeting in Clive's office and everyone was treated to some vicious language. Mr Limbrett explained what he had discovered and how he had stopped short of sacking everyone, not because of forgiveness or lack of evidence or any fear of reprisals, but simply because he could not muster up a sales team quickly enough to cope with the busy August period which was ahead. No one looked the others in the eye. Eyes were trained on boots. Salesmen were white with shock. Steve Limbrett was extremely angry. He slammed the door so hard he broke the lock. One thing was for sure after that: life at Spearlings would never be the same again.

And so it was. Clive was demoted from sales director to sales manager. Andre became senior salesman; both lost something. The accountants demanded new working practices and bit by bit, I think, Steve Limbrett played his new hand beautifully. We were beaten and there was not a thing to be done about it.

'Blimey, this is the third sale this month,' said Seth. 'It's getting like Allied Carpets.'

He was right. The new regime had brought in much more advertising with both the *Echo* and Stour Sound. Prices had been increased dramatically. Everyone had to see Tony, the finance manager. Every deal had to have a two-year warranty paid by the customer and the salesmen's commissions were lowered. Reconditioning costs were also deducted from the deal, so our pay suffered. Clive had lost his teeth – the accountants had won.

There was certainly more work to do now to earn your corn, but Spearlings was still a super place to earn money. The old guys were grumbling, but about things they shouldn't have. Some carried on harking for the old days and lads like Alan were still fiddling, but mainly a huge sigh of relief not to be sacked and a resigned acceptance of the status quo seemed to be the consensus of opinion.

*

'Leigh, you're working too hard!'

Although I'd known my wife Susan since school days she still insisted on using my surname. In fact, if she called me Mark it wasn't meant in an endearing way – I'd done something awful.

'I know, but you want a nice detached four-bed on a posh estate now, not in ten years' time.'

'But Mark, you need a holiday. You've been working seven days a week for months and all you talk about is cars.'

With that I knew this was the right moment to explain a lad from Grimley's was an avid sea fisherman who was arranging a trip for the next weekend. He needed eight lads and would organise the whole thing, including a minibus.

'What about life jackets?' was Sue's only response.

'On board – all taken care of,' I lied.

'Well, you go and enjoy it,' said Sue. 'It'll give me a chance to catch up with my sister that weekend.'

So that's why we finished early on Saturday. I'd persuaded Max to come too. Apparently he'd battled sea serpents and monsters off Swansea in his youth.

We changed, grabbed a small suitcase and drove around to Grimley's. The last of their customers were filtering away when I spotted Rocco the swarthy salesman. We spent the next hour collecting various lads from Loyworth, another suburb of Bradeley. All in all there were four sales lads from Spearlings and Grimley's and one lad who had a small 'back-street used car emporium'. He was called Rich.

Rocco collected two other lads from the Drake's Head. They rolled out twenty minutes after Rocco went into the bar. Both had cheery grins on their faces. Apparently both lads worked at the council as truck mechanics for the refuse department, hence their nicknames of 'Binman' and 'Smelly'. We were all honorary members of the Drake's Head Sea Angling Club, and were honour-bound to attend their monthly meetings.

'Anyway,' said Binman, 'where's the bait store?'

With that Rich cracked open the most tins of lager in a giant ice bucket I'd ever seen. Rich, Binman and

Smelly proceeded to get plastered on the long trip to Drewmouth by Sea.

Our hotel was hard to find. In fact it was a bed-and-breakfast within the George & Dragon pub, tucked away in a back street. Luckily it was still light. Bags were dropped in rooms and the landlady advised us that the best restaurant was to be found in the Crown Hotel.

As we entered it was obvious that we would push the boat out in this prestigious establishment. It was very much four-star and the middle floor of the three-storey hotel was given over to a silver service restaurant. All four sides were glass to give a superb panoramic view of the town, countryside and bay. You could hear a pin drop as we took our seats at the large central table. The restaurant was almost full and apart from light coughing, chairs moving on the wooden floorboards and polite requests for orders from the waiters, it was quiet.

The four waiters were dressed in traditional black suits and waistcoats with patent leather shoes. Each one had a name tag on their lapel. Our 'Mario' was very attentive. He was also camp and minced between order and kitchen like a peacock.

Our starters all arrived at once and all four waiters worked swiftly to ensure maximum efficiency. The restaurant was an orchestra of tinkling knives, forks, plates and glasses when Binman picked up the *Sun*, turned to page three and announced, 'Cor, I'd rather be up her than upset!' The room stopped and thirty-two pairs of eyes stared at Binman. It was like being frozen in time for an age. All the time I think he was totally oblivious to what he had done.

The morning brought heavy heads. George, the landlord of the George & Dragon, had stayed up till two in the morning with the lads to discuss all things pub. Julian, one of Grimley's lads, was a former publican, therefore pipe cleaning, stock control and barrel sizes came up in the conversation. George was bright and cheery, so too Smelly, but the rest of us made a sullen crew.

We met the skipper at the harbour at 8.45am. He brought bait and lines; we rolled on board. Rocco had brought rolls, ham and cheese, crisps and other provisions.

'Looks like a good fishing day, boys,' he said. 'We'll just aim out for the wrecks – an hour's steaming away. Put some mackerel lines down.'

We soon got into the shoals of mackerel; it was hardly skilful fishing but good fun. The rest of the day was a mixture of quiet recovery for some and gentle fun for others. A selection of dogfish, ray, conger eels and sea bass filled one of three buckets the skipper had provided. Two of the boys were decidedly yellow in colour. Julian spent the entire day over the side providing ground bait for the English Channel.

The highlight of the day was my arm-wrenching challenge of pulling in what seemed to be a London bus. Eventually I saw the silver back of an enormous fish.

'Get the net on that one,' shouted the skipper. 'That's too nice a fish to lose!'

When we inspected and weighed it, it was a three-foot-long 18lb ling. That was the fish of the day, and it and I were hooked.

After several liveners in the Mermaid and a superb evening meal, the boys were in great spirits. However, packing away the fish and an early morning start awaited. Work was calling in the morning.

Back to the grind of daily activity, customer complaints, cars not ready to be delivered and cancellations.

'You've lost your job and fallen out of an apple tree and broken your leg, all in one afternoon? Wow, Mr Whitehead, you've been unlucky.' Alan's mock sympathy was belied by the utter sarcasm in his voice. 'That's taken the record. Until now the best one was "We've just had the electricity bill in and I think it's for the whole street, so I can't go ahead with the car, Mr Rooney"!'

Alan slammed the phone down, muttering away about the illogical nature of Joe Public, amongst swearing and cussing. Buyer's remorse was a common byproduct of the retail motor trade. Arguments at home with family or an innocent remark in the pub often led to a cooling of the desire that had been skilfully conjured by a hard-working salesman. There was always an expert in the pub who, made jealous by poverty, would spoil a prospective purchase by planting seeds of doubt in his 'friend's' mind. *I had one of those a couple of years ago, nothing but trouble. In the repair shop more than on the road, it was!* These guys were spiteful, ignorant fools, but the damage was done and the deal called off.

'Let's fight the case,' I said to Andre. 'We've got a signed order and I spent three days with that family, only for some idiot in a pub to ruin the sale.'

'It's not worth it, Mark. We're the professionals, and if it went to Trading Standards you'd lose and suffer bad publicity in the *Echo*. Just put the car back up for sale and chalk it down to experience!'

Off I went in a huff, the day spoilt, and any trust in the word of customers took another blow.

Talking about this subject during our Saturday evening drinks club meeting, I asked Max how he managed to attend. I knew his wife to be, in Jeff's words, 'a right battleaxe'.

'Oh, that's easy,' said Max. 'For over twenty-five years I've told her, "PU meeting tonight, love, I'll be late in." It was only a couple of months ago I let slip "PU" was short for "piss-up" when we all went on that fishing trip.' The penny had dropped, but surprisingly his wife had just chuckled and carried on watching her soap opera.

'What do you do if someone cancels an order on you, Max?' I asked.

He explained that nowadays he dealt with mainly old established customers, their friends and family or people recommended to him. Therefore he didn't have such a problem as the younger lads starting out. However, years ago he'd had a muffie who owned a fish and chip shop on Muffleyford High Street. This guy was hard work but eventually bought a Montego that had been in stock since Adam was a lad. The day before collection Max received a phone call from a very downhearted chip shop owner who explained that he couldn't go ahead with the transaction because he'd had a major fire in his shop and he wasn't insured.

'Wow, that's one of the best excuses I've ever heard,'

Max had retorted angrily, slamming down the phone and questioning the parentage of one of Muffleyford's finest.

'But Mark,' said Max, 'just imagine how I felt when that night I picked up the *Echo* and the headlines were "Fire destroys local takeaway". To read about my customer's catastrophe with a picture of him and his shop: it nearly made me feel sorry for him!'

*

The coming months produced more fun, more laughs and plenty of hard work for the Spearlings sales team. However, endless meetings, men in grey suits and long faces from Clive and Andre meant trouble in the air. Rumours spread amongst all the staff and gossip was rife.

'I'm telling you we've gone bust!' said Tony the finance man. 'I can spot a bailiff a hundred yards away.'

'Don't be daft,' said Seth. 'How could we be bust? It's been a record year for sales.'

Whatever the reason for all the meetings, life at Spearlings would never be the same again.

Earlier that year Alan Rooney had found premises less than half a mile away and set up AR Autos, a used car establishment catering for the cheaper end of the market. He'd taken Robbie Stevens with him. They were very close and shared an eccentric view of business and life that seemed to work for their new venture. The fact that neither salesman had been replaced only fed the rumour mill. Certainly Alan in particular was badly missed by Clive.

Over the following weeks strange events began to happen. Garages and trailers appeared. Odd-looking drivers were summoned into Clive's office and fresh used cars, prime stock, were taken away. When the salesmen objected, all Clive or Andre would say was 'Head office orders. We need to reduce stock before the tax year ends.'

Transporters arrived and took saleable used cars to auction. The salesmen were spending their days loading transporters with the very cars they should be selling to make their living. There was a lot of crying into beer and bemoaning the situation. Rumours abounded throughout Spearlings because not only sales but all the departments were returning stock or downsizing their operation.

Eventually we were informed by Clive in a special late meeting that Spearlings was being sold by the finance house that owned it to a Scotland-based motor group who were expanding their operation in the south. All jobs were safe, the group was run by an astute financial guru. It would be business as usual with a fresh input of capital and few changes!

'You wait,' said Jeff. 'They'll just do an asset-stripping job and ditch the non-profit-making areas of the business. I've seen it done before when accountants and money men get involved with a family-run business. It's the end of Spearlings as we know it. Prepare for heavy changes!'

Those words kept ringing through my brain, and in the coming weeks things did change.

'Right, boys,' said Clive, 'you're having a new uniform!'

Groans, moans and grumbles.

'Here you are: green blazer, white short-sleeved shirt and grey slacks.'

'I'm not wearing that crap,' said Seth. 'I'm too old to look like a spotty school kid.'

The green blazer was smart enough, but the whole of the top pocket was covered by a vulgar badge with 'Motorway City' printed in large red letters. The shirt and grey trousers were made from the cheapest, nastiest polyester that a Vietnamese sweatshop could produce.

'I keep getting electric shocks when I sit down,' said Tommy.

'And these shirts just bite your neck and armpits,' Charlie piped in.

'We all look like we've changed jobs – Spearlings coach driver!' I said.

It raised the only laugh of the day.

Over the coming weeks new stock arrived to fill the empty forecourt spaces. There was a strange mixture of high-mileage ex-lease cars, many being of high-end quality makes, and nearly new ex-rental vehicles. Max Williams was excited by the quality vehicles but it was obvious many were of dubious origin.

'They're all dodgy with no service history. They've come from a Glasgow auction and seem pretty rough to me!' said Seth.

The nearly new Fiestas and Escorts cleaned up quite well and when an old customer came in looking to upgrade his Fiesta, I had no hesitation in selling him a silver model. A day later my customer sheepishly approached me, asking for a quiet word.

'Mark, I don't like to complain, but I took the Fiesta to my local garage to have it checked out. They didn't believe the mileage, so I phoned the previous owner – Maller Rent-a-Car in Glasgow. When I asked him what the mileage was he said, "Fuck off!" So, Mark, I want my money back.'

We checked all the cars. Many were formerly of Maller Rent-a-Car and had been clocked, and some were write-offs. One Sierra had a Transit engine and wouldn't start. The exotic vehicles were all clocked. One Mazda cabriolet was made up from three vehicles. It was a horror story!

Clive and Andre just buried their heads and told us to sell the stock and avoid rocking the boat. Of course, that's exactly what I didn't do. Customers weren't fooled. They did not like the Glasgow registration plates or the types of car that were on display. Our local rivals had a field day. Their sales rocketed on the back of our misfortune.

'What can we do, Max?' I asked. 'This can't go on! Quite apart from not earning, it's so blooming boring sat here in these stupid clothes. The highlight of the day is what's for lunch.'

'I know,' he said, 'but something will break. Clive and Andre are under far more pressure than us to move tin!'

But nothing did break, and weeks turned into months. The sales staff's morale was lower than a snake's belly.

'Mark, come into my car,' ordered Max one day.

In the car, he spoke with a serious tone to his voice I'd never heard before. 'This place has had it! Spearlings will never be the same again. Any good salesmen will leave and be replaced by dross. You've got to face facts like me, 'cause if you stay here you'll either starve or become a crook!'

The last part of the sentence hit home. It was what I had been fretting over for weeks.

'These people are Glasgow wide boys,' said Max. 'I bet they have connections with the underworld. At best they're very shady. This is what the motor trade was like years ago, before trading standards and legislation cleaned it up and made it a proper profession. I for one don't want any part of this set-up.'

'But what can we do, Max?' I asked.

'Well, that's what I want to talk about.'

We spent the next two hours reviewing our options. Finally, head spinning, I'd come to the conclusion that I didn't wish to find another job at a rival dealership. I would join Max and find our own used car operation. Now all I had to do was sell the idea to Susan, find premises and capital and start a new business.

The next few weeks were a whirlwind of activity. Even if sales were very slow, Max and I had to look as though we were busy championing Spearlings' cause. Favours were called in and banter was much in evidence. Everything had to look normal.

Susan had taken the news badly at first. She was a very cautious lady with working-class ideals. Owning your own business was for 'posh people' and I shouldn't have ideas above my station. However, with Max's wise words and my constant updates on how intolerable the new people were to work for, she was slowly relenting.

News of the premises came from a very unlikely source: Clive Laidlaw. I'd gone to get my hair cut and there was Clive in the barber's chair, talking to Clint Sargerson, at the local men's clip joint.

'Remember your first job in the motor trade, Clive?' Clint asked. 'Well, I hear that old yard will be back on the market soon!'

'Oh,' said Clive, 'what's happened to the tile shop that's there now?'

'Gone bust, I hear,' said Clint. 'The son that's running it has got a big gambling problem and owes the local bookies over £100,000. Rumour has it that Fedwest bank has pulled the plug and sequestrated the mortgage. Put the property in the hands of Harry Edwards of Edwards and Partners to sell or lease. He was in yesterday and was telling me all about it. The mother is devastated. Three generations built the business up, for the son to blow it all on the nags! What's happening at your place, Clive?'

'Oh, it's murder, Clint, talk about a pickle. I'm surrounded by crooked owners and disgruntled staff. I've only got three years until my pension, so I have to see it through and take orders, but it's tough. Do you know, Clint, these Glasgow boys are something else. Even Ali Baba only had forty thieves!'

I left to the sound of guffaws. They didn't see me because the waiting room was down from Clint's chair.

I don't know what intrigued Max more: news of the premises or the revelation that Clive had taken the Scots' instructions against all his principles.

'Well, that's put the tin hat on it,' said Max. 'If you were in any doubt before, now you know working for Spearlings is like being in a gangster's den. Anyway, I've spoken to Harry Edwards and we've got a meet on Friday, 12.30 sharp – look smart.'

Apparently Max supplied Harry and his business with cars. 'I've known him for years and we're in the same Rotary Lodge. He wanted to know how we knew about the Turnbull's Tiles site coming on the market.'

'That's easy, Max,' I said. 'Obviously it leaked from the bookies how much Jim Turnbull owed. We then just added two and two.'

'Mark,' said Max, 'that's brilliant – I'll make a Welshman of you yet!'

Discussions with Harry Edwards went well. It helped that Max knew him well and we cut to the chase quickly. Harry managed to wheedle the minimum rent Fedwest would accept, together with a five-year lease figure with an option to purchase in year six. Everything was in place except financing.

'Try another bank first,' said Harry. 'You're better off not having a landlord as your banker – too much control!'

'That's awkward,' said Max. 'I know Fedwest well, it's my own bank, plus I'm in with the undermanager at Bradeley's top branch.'

I was beginning to realise Max was a very useful partner. His connections locally were to be invaluable. We worked out figures on the back of a fag packet. The rent and rates were steep but achievable. Money for office refurbishment and stock, now, that's where the problem lay.

The business plan we drew up between us was better fiction than *Star Wars*. The figures were drawn from what the accountants and bean counters at the bank wanted to hear. We managed to secure an interview at Grant LSC bank for a business start-up package. The bank would match pound for pound what we could raise from savings.

Mr Leather, the appointed business manager, read out the rules of engagement. He swallowed our business plan and projections and seemed impressed with Max's well-rehearsed spiel. Max had a £15,000 pot saved mainly for his pension fund. I had about 10% of that as emergency savings.

'No remortgaging to raise extra funds, boys,' said Mr Leather.

We both looked at each other, knowing full well that was the only route we had for start-up and stock.

'That went well,' said Max, afterwards, 'but the rent and lease are going to swallow half of our ready cash. We have to raise money for stock and although Turnbull's Tiles will make a great car pitch, we'll need to spend money on signage, security and office refurb.'

I was miles away, not really listening to the steady lilt of Max's voice. I was trying to think of a way to approach Susan about refinancing the equity in our home to start what she would view as a risky business selling second-hand cars.

After many sleepless nights, tears and tantrums from Susan and numerous visits from Max, we eventually thrashed out our own business plan. Max was brilliant. Although he put in most of the money and had all the business knowledge, he insisted that we be equal partners and that he only wanted five years, after which I could buy him out at a favourable price for that time. Susan got her new kitchen and holiday of a lifetime and the die was cast.

'Max Value Cars'. The signs looked bold in bright yellow and black. We had decided to trade on Max's name. All our launch advertising was built around his experience and popularity in the Bradeley area. The site looked good with its fresh tarmac, laid by some enterprising gypsies who just 'happened to have some left over from a big job'. The office was refurbished and two luxury desks and chairs were the only new indulgence. Everything else was second-hand, charity shop or gifted to us. The only thing we lacked was a stock of cars! The site would hold fifty-plus vehicles. We had scraped together eight from family and friends and what was left of our budget.

'How are we going to fill this place, lovely boy?' asked Max.

I just shrugged my shoulders. 'What did Alan and Robbie do to stock their pitch?'

'Let's go see!' said Max.

*

AR Autos. The fluorescent sign hummed in the still air. A converted railway carriage made a scruffy office. The tarmac was pitted and dishevelled and full of tall weeds. Rubbish and burger cartons littered the hedgerow. However, the forecourt was full of gleaming cars. I caught sight of Alan, and a big grin was followed by hugs all round.

'Come in, grab a coffee, mind the mess, park your bum!' A machine-gun volley of commands.

'Where's Robbie?' Max asked.

'Oh, delivering a convertible to some bored housewife he's been chasing. He's only been gone two hours. Might see him back before close of play!'

Max swore Alan to secrecy about our plans, but we were both shocked to find he already knew.

'Can't keep a secret in the Bradeley motor trade

mafia, boys!' he said. 'You were spotted sniffing around the old tile shop premises. Must admit, it'll make a good site. Always worked as a garage years ago.'

'But who told you?' I asked.

'Harry Edwards,' said Alan. 'Once he's had a few chasers in the Lion he just has to boast about his sales for the day. I've known for weeks!'

'Oh,' said Max. 'Well, that makes what we've got to ask you even more urgent.'

Max went on to explain our predicament.

'Ah, same problem I had when we started up! You've got three choices, boys. One: scratch round for cheap and nasty cars to fill the site. Two: get more into debt with a stock purchase plan with a second-string lender and pay eye-watering interest, or three: find a motor dealer who will do SOR.'

'What's that?' I naively asked.

'SOR means "sale or return" – you find someone who provides stock they own, who tells you what they want back for the cars. You put your margin on top, own the part-exchange and deal with the customer from start to finish. Oh, there is another option,' chirped Alan. 'Win the pools!'

'Ha ha, very funny, but where do you find someone like that?' I asked.

'Well, we did; where do you think all those came from?' he said, pointing to his stock. 'Spearlings never paid that well! You'll be surprised how many car traders put cars on other people's sites. Just be careful who you get into bed with!'

With that Alan spotted an old boy looking at a car

and was off with a 'Can I help you at all?' at the top of his voice.

Max was beaming from ear to ear. 'Wow, what a perfect solution. We're bound to know someone to stock us and we've just enough cash to buy the part-exchanges. Anyway, let's get back to work. Don't want the sack just yet, boyo!'

The truth was we needed to work at Spearlings for one more week to be sure of our pay for a busy August. We didn't trust the new people.

'My office, you two – now,' boomed Clive. 'What's this about you reopening my old garage at Turnbull's?'

He slammed the door so all three of us were inches apart.

'It's true,' said Max, 'and if you had any sense you'd come with us.'

'Oh, I wish, but you'd better both keep away. Get signed off by your doctor or whatever, but keep away, and I'll make sure the Glasgow mafia don't get wind or you'll never see your August commission cheques!'

'That was good of Clive,' I said, as we left his office.

'Least he could do,' said Max. 'I feel sorry for Clive, three years at least with the Glasgow gangsters before he can escape. Anyway, you go on that super holiday of yours, Mark, and when you come back prepare for some hard work and fun.'

Chapter 4

Two weeks later Sue and I returned to a rainy old England. The time in Mauritius had been fabulous. We were de-stressed and horizontal for the fortnight. I'd just completed the last interesting crime novel from the hotel's library. Collecting our bags at Heathrow brought thoughts of Max and a tinge of conscience that he was beavering away at our new venture.

'You start unpacking, Sue, and I'll just nip to see Max and catch up!' I slammed the front door before she could answer.

*

'Wow, Max, everything's looking great,' I lied, thinking the bunting and flags were very garish. 'I see you've got shares in the bunting factory!'

'Cheek, I'll have you know they were a bargain. Do you like my flags, holiday boy?'

Max brought me up to speed; he'd sold his first car and traded an Escort that wasn't quite retail quality. People had been venturing in to see what was happening and, of course, Max loved his role as convivial host. The big problem was to fill the site with quality cars. He explained that he had approached several traders but getting someone who would be compatible was not proving easy.

'Plenty are shady or downright crooks and liars,' he intoned.

Some wanted far too much of a return on their stock. Others were out of tune with our sales philosophy. They thought scruffy, high-mileage cars would be saleable. However, through a Rotary contact Max had found an old-school motor trader who had just sold his retail car business. He wasn't ready to retire completely and might be keen to mentor a new venture. We were to meet him at his house the next evening.

When we arrived at Jack Hart's country mansion we thought we'd got the wrong address. A big meaty hand was extended and a broad smile beamed at us.

'Evening, gentlemen. Please do come in.'

The house was out of *Country Homes* and Jack was sartorial elegance personified. Three hours later, fuelled with fine cognac, Max and I drove away from the gravelled drive grinning from ear to ear.

'We've hit the jackpot here, Max,' I ventured.

'Aye, boyo, but let's just get home in one piece. We'll talk about it in the morning.'

Next day, through bleary eyes and a thumping head, Max and I pieced together our meeting with Jack. He would supply three-to-five-year-old family-based cars, ex-lease, which for the past twenty years had been the cornerstone of his garage and car sales business. He would deliver them to our site and furnish us with the registration document, MOT, sales history and keys. We were expected to cover any minor mechanical and paintwork problems, valet the car and sort out any ongoing warranty issues. He would agree with us a figure he expected back, which he assured us would be fair and would reflect his investment. 'I know you boys have to earn,' was his explanation.

There would be no time limit on days in stock before being sold – but obviously Jack could withdraw his car at any time if no sale was forthcoming. We would also be responsible for insuring and maintaining the appearance of his stock, and all advertising.

'I've had enough of retail, boys; time to give wholesale a go!' was how he explained his thinking.

'I might have a fuzzy head, Max,' I said, 'but I can't see any problems, can you?'

'Well, that's the first thing you did wrong, young man,' said Max sternly. 'Lesson number one: never let traders ply you with drink. It's the oldest trick in their book to sneak through a dodgy motor or deal. However, I think Jack's straight enough.' He looked worried. 'I'd just love to know where he sources his cars.'

'But surely that's what he's built up all these years, and anyway how can we worry about that?'

'That's just what we have to worry about!' Max seemed angry. 'Just remember, Mark, these lads are looking after number one and you don't get a country pile like that by being completely straight and honest!'

It was agreed that we had little choice but to trust Jack and agree with his terms. 'Beggars and choosers' became a well-worn phrase. We phoned Jack, who sounded pleased, and we invited him to our premises that afternoon. He seemed delighted with everything and, of course, he remembered the garage from years ago, so he and Max regaled each other with stories and characters from a bygone age.

The first transporter load of cars arrived three days later. 'Five for you,' shouted the driver as he reversed the first blue Vauxhall onto the pavement. It smelt a little musty and needed a thorough clean, but generally it was sound. The four others were of a similar standard. We had them cleaned. Jack told us his 'stand-in' price; we added our margin and priced them accordingly. Over the following week, with careful positioning, we managed to make the site look appealing and slowly the general public sheepishly wandered in, wondering what was going on.

After two weeks we had only sold one car, to a friend of Max, and we were both beginning to twitch.

'What we need is a launch,' said Max.

'Huh? What do you mean?' I replied.

'Get the press down and get things in the local paper. Tell 'em we've arrived! You've got to let 'em know what's happening!'

So that's how things began to take off. After a midweek double-page spread in the *Bradeley Echo*, footfall slowly improved. The weekly advertising was expensive but effective. Soon we had sold twenty-odd cars in three weeks. Everyone was happy and Jack was a regular visitor. He'd increased his car total to nearly forty, so he was keen to be paid as soon as a car was delivered.

'He must have a camera in the office to know what's happening,' said Max.

'He's here for hours most days, don't forget, and he spots delivery times on our orders,' I replied.

'Yeah, no flies on Jack,' Max chuckled as he passed by.

Over the following weeks and months we had a steady flow of advertising, finance and warranty reps all trying to sell their products.

'Leave them to me,' said Max. 'You're too gullible, especially to a pretty face.'

It was true; I was a sucker for a well-rehearsed line to entice us to spend more money. The advertising reps especially must have been recruited on their looks alone. Always female and flirty. Robbie at AR Autos must have had a field day.

The first six months went well with a steady if unspectacular level of business. We were making a profit and the bank was happy. Jack seemed pleased with his investment and Susan was happy in her role of bookkeeper, helping with all things accounts-wise.

We found a finance house that would advance 90% of the screen price. This was a godsend because we could legitimately advertise this with a weekly equivalent of, say, £24.95. Far better than £3,000 balance over forty-eight months. With commission paid on top we found people just didn't haggle with the price. Therefore, the next twelve months of trading showed a healthy profit.

We were celebrating this first birthday when our first real setback occurred. I noticed the paintwork on the bonnets across the front row looked frosted. On closer inspection it became obvious that all the paint had bubbled up.

'Paint stripper,' said Max. 'What a mess. How many have they done?'

'The front six,' I replied.

'Phone the insurance company and I'll move them out the back,' said Max tensely.

The insurance company couldn't have been more helpful, but each car had an excess of £200.

'Don't worry,' said Brian at B & K bodyshop, 'I'll bump up the estimates to cover some of the excess, and I'll get the boys on overtime to get 'em back this week. Who was it? Kids, or have you upset anyone?'

This opened a great debate between Max, Jack and me.

'We've not made any enemies,' I said.

'Huh, when you're a success you'd be surprised how many people become envious. It's the British disease. They hate winners and they'll do anything to make you a loser out of sheer spite,' Max said cynically.

'Max's right,' said Jack. 'I had my pitch done five or six times over the first ten years. The last time I stayed up all night for a month, slept during the day. Caught 'em, like. It was a local roughneck employed by a so-called friendly rival. However hard I twisted his arm he wouldn't admit it, though. Police just gave him a caution – couldn't prove it.' He shook his head in disgust. 'My word against his.'

'What did you do?' asked Max.

'Oh, I waited a couple of months and then did some serious paint removal, only it wasn't one or two – it was the whole garage! No one beats Jack Hart,' he said coldly. 'Never happened again either. You gotta fight fire with fire.'

When he'd gone Max and I scratched our heads as to who it might have been.

'It's either yobs or the Glasgow geeks,' said Max.

'But why would they be vindictive to us? We don't come anywhere near their league!' I said.

'I don't know,' said Max, 'but it sure makes you sick to the stomach to know there are people capable ..' He tailed off, shaking his head at the thought.

We never did find out who vandalised our cars, but an educated guess led us back to our former employers. Why they thought to do such a thing was a mystery, though.

The winter months dragged along and business was slow and steady, buoyed by our finance business. We had a few setbacks. A couple of cars developed major faults and a break-in was upsetting, but generally business life was good.

Christmas came and went and soon we entered the new year. We had made enough money to stock twenty-five cars from part-exchanges and local purchases. Soon it was time to enter the mysterious world of the used car auction. Max had a little experience of auctions but I was a complete novice. Therefore, it was agreed that Max would accompany Jack to the next sale at Birmingham on Thursday.

'Don't buy any lemons,' I shouted to Max as he jumped in the back seat of Jack's Audi estate. Jack was driving; next to him in the front was Tom, one of Jack's trade cronies, who also helped drive and massage Jack's enormous ego.

Just on closing time I watched as Max tottered out of the Audi. As he came closer I noticed that he was as white as a sheet and his hands shook.

'What's up, Max? You seen a ghost?' I enquired.

'Worse than that, man, I've just been driven 150 miles

by a maniac. I will never, ever drive with that man again.' He then regaled me with the events of the day. 'He just drove from the slip road straight across three lanes, into the fast lane at 115 miles an hour. He never dropped below a hundred, all the time looking at Tom or me and storytelling or laughing. I closed my eyes or looked out of the side window and prayed to myself.'

Max had bought two cars, Cliff four, so a transporter would arrive presently.

'Your turn next time, Mark, and you're welcome to it!' was all Max would say as he got into his car and gingerly set off home.

The next two weeks produced an upturn in business. We'd sold fifteen cars and there were several gaps which needed filling, so when Jack suggested another outing to the car auction at Walsall I didn't hesitate. Armed with a list of cars for prospective customers, I checked my jacket for car guide, cheque book, notepad and pen.

'Got your nerve pills, boyo? You'll need them!' whispered Max with a knowing grin.

'He can't be that bad. Anyway, looks like there's only two of us, no Tom!'

Well, it was that bad; in fact it was worse. Jack drove like a maniac, shouting and cursing anyone in his way. He tailgated anyone in the outside lane who wasn't driving at the speed of light, flashing his lights until, intimidated, they pulled over. My feet were pressed into the passenger footwell, standing on the imaginary brake pedal. I took Max's advice and looked out of the side window, colour drained from my face. I tried to reassure myself with the thought that Jack wouldn't want to die. However, what if he had a tyre blowout at that speed? No wonder Max had prayed!

The auction proved bewildering – so many cars, different mileages and ages, and they seemed to be sold before I knew what was happening. I'd spotted a blue Ford Sierra which on closer inspection seemed a good buy. My heart was thumping out of my chest as it came in front of the rostrum. The bidding started and a blur of seconds later I raised my hand, the hammer fell, the auctioneer pointed at me and I'd bought my first auction car.

'Blimey, that was cheap,' I muttered under my breath. It was only after the end of the sale that I realised why. The Sierra I'd wanted had done 39,000 miles and this one had done 79,000. Oops! Oh well, I thought, at least it was £600 cheaper than the guide price!

The customer I had in mind was very understanding when I presented the vehicle, freshly valeted, days later. It drove nicely and at £500 less than anticipated he bought it. Phew! I wouldn't make that mistake again.

Oh, and by the way, I never drove in the same car as Jack again. Driving back through Birmingham's Five Ways, he drove past a red light; a car swerved to avoid us and just missed a parked vehicle. To this day he is completely oblivious to what he did!

*

Life at Max Value Cars went along in a mundane, humdrum way. However, Max and I both noticed that Jack's purchases were beginning to get both more expensive and more average than when we had first started. Max and I agreed that Jack was obviously supplying other garages with better quality stock.

'We're getting the dregs,' Max said. 'We'll just have to buy our own. We've got more money in the bank and I know plenty of traders and sales managers who'd supply. Just don't broadcast it; we can't afford to upset Jack just yet.'

But upset Jack we did. We bought some of our own cars, purposely avoiding the make and models Jack favoured. When we were quizzed, they were always part-exchanges or cars we were selling on behalf of friends and family. However, Jack was not stupid or gullible and his moody, sulky silences for weeks on end lay heavy, forecasting storms ahead.

*

'Hey, Max, look at that punter on the pitch.' We played a game of prediction and scale as to whether the customers were 'hands up', i.e. ready to surrender easily to the purchase, or, at the other extreme, tyre killers or timewasters.

'He's a five-star tyre killer,' said Max.

'How do you work that out?' I asked.

'Well, boyo, my first sales manager Bill Morgan reckoned anyone with a beard was hard work. Anyone who smoked a pipe couldn't make up their mind in a month of Sundays, and anyone who wore sandals in winter belonged to the Moonies. Just look at him!'

'Oh my God,' I said. 'He's got a big bushy ginger beard, he's smoking a pipe and there's frost on the ground but he's wearing Jesus sandals! Still, I bet I can sell him a car.'

'Ten pounds says you won't.'

'You're on,' I shouted from across the forecourt.

Three hours and five test drives later I conceded

defeat. Not a glimmer of enthusiasm, not a word of positive feedback – nothing.

'Here's the tenner I owe you, Max. Oh and by the way, if you see another punter like that you've got my permission to shoot him, or me, to put one of us out of our misery!'

*

We'd become friendly with the local Midwest Auto Finance company. The manager Roger Faraday and his two young reps were really friendly, accommodating and helpful. Nothing was too much trouble and many strings were pulled to get finance deals and advances through.

'Come on, Mark, fill in an entry form and it'll go into a prize draw. Look at the prizes,' said Alex, one of the young enthusiastic reps.

'Bah, I've never won so much as a church raffle,' I said. 'What makes you think I'm going to win a national competition?'

'Just sign the bottom of the entry form,' he said. 'I'll fill in all the details of the car and customer.'

I hardly bothered looking at the prizes but noted a £200 video machine and minor prizes that looked like I wouldn't have to bother Christmas shopping for Sue.

Winter had set in and the winter blues were beginning to show. Few sales but lots of screamers. The harsh weather always caught out poor batteries or service-based car problems that customers wanted the garage to pay for. It was on just such a boringly quiet afternoon that I received a call from a very excitable Mr Faraday.

'You'd better sit down,' he said.

I could tell it wasn't bad news but I was in no mood

for a wind-up, which were prevalent in the quiet winter months.

'Yeah, Rog, what have I done this time?' I asked.

'You've only bloody won the star prize in the competition.'

'Yeah, yeah, and they've just spotted Lord Lucan on a red London bus!'

'No – you have, Mark—'

I dropped the phone down, recognising a wind-up. Then, seconds later, the phone rang again. Something in Roger's voice made me hesitate; however, Roger had been a master of kidology in the past.

'I'm not in the mood, Rog.' With that I dropped the phone again.

Half an hour later a polished voice who introduced himself as a director of Midwest Auto Finance plc. informed me that we had been selected in their national finance campaign as the winners of the star prize – a trip on Cunard's *Queen Elizabeth 2* to New York with a return on Concorde. Wow. I found Max and we did a jig around the office.

We purposely sold most of the cars we had bought ourselves during the next six weeks. Few of Jack's sold, but enough to keep him on reasonable terms.

What we couldn't decide on was who should benefit from this prize. There were two tickets. Max wanted Sue and me to benefit but we wouldn't hear of it. We phoned Cunard but two extra tickets for the girls would be £4,500 each, money we didn't have. We were on the horns of a dilemma.

'What should we do?' I asked Jack after explaining the predicament.

'Hmm, well, apart from spinning a coin, you two started the business together and won the prize together, so you've got to take the trip together! I'll man the office for the ten days; it's December, so it can't be that busy. The girls will just have to lump it.'

I asked Sue what she would be happy with, and surprisingly she agreed with Jack. 'I had a wonderful holiday in Mauritius last year, so you and Max have to go!'

So it was decided. However, Max played his 'I won't fly and I haven't a passport' trick, so I told him we'd just forfeit the whole thing. His Welsh meanness came out and he decided to take the road to Newport, sort out his passport, grit his teeth and realise a trip on Concorde was once in his lifetime. Not before making everyone aware of the great hardship it was all going to be.

Jack kept his promise to man the fort for the ten-day jolly. We gave him the keys and made arrangements to embark on an adventure which was to change the shape of our lives forever.

Max hired a chauffeur who collected us from our homes and took us to Southampton. When we collected Max he appeared with his suitcase, dressed to the nines in an expensive suit, highly polished shoes and a Granby overcoat, looking every inch the sartorial man of the world.

'Got to look the part for those Yanks,' he said.

Max was certainly embracing the whole experience!

To say I saw another side to Max in the next few weeks would be a massive understatement. As soon as he jumped from the gangplank and onto the cruise ship he was that five-year-old boy who woke on Christmas morning to a whole pile of presents! His eyes were saucers and his only vocabulary was 'wow'.

We dumped our bags in our stateroom and then toured the liner. Designer shops, chandeliers, smartly uniformed staff, plus restaurants, elegant ballrooms and casinos with flashing lights. It became a blur of opulence and luxury which Max seemed hypnotised by.

'Slow down, Max, we've got five days of this Atlantic crossing. There's plenty of time to see and do everything on your list.'

I may as well have spoken to a Honduran waiter who spoke no English and just grinned at everything you said to him.

We dressed for dinner and found six other Brits who shared our table. Introductions and small talk were exchanged and a superb three-course meal was enjoyed. My neighbouring diner was a pleasant older lady from the Home Counties who, together with a friend, was treating herself after a traumatic year following the death of her husband. Max was the life and soul of the table, regaling us with stories from his early years in Wales.

'Let's sample the disco, boyo!'

It was more in the way of a command than a request. We didn't bother to change and joined the hardy souls in the ballroom in the bowels of the vessel. The Atlantic in December meant all but the most hardy partygoer retired to their cabins after dinner. Dancing on the disco floor wasn't necessary because the swell of the Atlantic formed our steps and movement.

The disco was very dark and loud. I sat and ordered

drinks, luxuriating in my leather chair, observing and man-watching. I noticed Max's head bobbing from table to table as he engaged with our various fellow travellers.

After a couple of hours I'd had enough. It had been a long day and the alcohol was taking its toll. I arranged to leave the cabin door open and left Max chatting to a table of ladies. He was in mid-flow and his element. 'Lightweight' was his only comment as I climbed the stairs and found our stateroom.

*

The drone of the ship's engines stirred my head. I could hear people in the corridor. The light from the porthole and the view of the sea on the television monitor told me it was the morning, but something felt missing. That something was Max. His bed had not been slept in!

As I readied myself in the bathroom a dishevelled figure appeared, bleary-eyed and a little sheepish.

'Oh, the wanderer returns. Must have been a good party.'

'I'll tell you later. Right now I want some breakfast; I'm starving.'

Max was like a child. The variety of breakfast food was amazing. He tried every type of bacon and sausage on display, finishing with croissants and coffee!

Max couldn't wait to relay his adventures of his first night. It transpired that he had chanced upon a group of lady travel agents who worked for a large American holiday chain that specialised in upmarket cruise adventures. Cunard had funded a free cruise for these agents in return for their marketing the QE2's delights.

'What a laugh we had,' said Max.

'But not all night, surely, Max?' I asked.

At this Max blushed and waffled effusively about a Claudia from Chicago who he was meeting for lunch.

For the next two days I didn't see Max. It was very embarrassing hanging around the bars or staying in the cabin, watching videos or reading a book borrowed from the Cunard library. I dressed for dinner and met my fellow Brits, who noted the empty chair. I made excuses for Max and said he wasn't feeling well. However, my dinner neighbour mentioned seeing Max with a tall American lady on deck.

'They were laughing and giggling and having a wonderful time,' she said.

'Oh,' I said and quickly changed the subject, quietly seething as I wondered what Max was playing at!

Later, when he came back to the cabin, I confronted him. He was in no mood for my questions and stated in no uncertain terms that he would do what he liked with whom he liked. It was his holiday and he would spend it with Claudia. I should put up, shut up and find someone – a lady – to enjoy it with! This was a nasty, selfish side of Max I had not seen before and did not like.

Luckily the crossing became rougher to the point of being stormy. The queue outside the doctor's waiting room grew longer as he dispensed sea sickness pills or injections at £50 per time, making a tidy profit. People confined themselves to their cabins for meals. The dining room resembled a game of 'spot the customer' until finally the last day arrived and we closed in on the east coast of America.

I awoke early on the final day and joined a throng of

passengers to see in the arrival at New York. Past the Statue of Liberty, into the vastness of the harbourside. What a sight for all those newcomers to this wonderful land. Farewells were said and eventually we disembarked the beautiful craft which was the QE2.

I found the coach which was to take us to our hotel in New York. The city was a thriving mass of activity. Stretch limos and yellow cabs buzzed around the harbourside like bees. Max was the last person to alight from the coach. We dropped off fellow travellers at their various hotels and eventually drew up to the Waldorf Astoria.

The hotel had the biggest foyer I'd ever seen. It was large and grand and anonymous. Max and I collected the room keys, found the lift and in silence found room 1197.

Max tried to act as if nothing had happened. He returned to his old friendly bubbling self, but the damage had been done. When I tried to explain how rude, selfish and embarrassing he'd been he tried to brush it off.

'Just a bit of fun, boyo; that's what holidays are for!'

I began to question myself, such was his conviction. At this juncture I decided to leave the past five days behind and enjoy the rest of the holiday.

New York in December is freezing. Snow and ice cover the 'sidewalks' and the icy wind from the Hudson River cuts you in two. We did the usual touristy trips but Max was in a different world to mine. He became sullen and withdrawn and very poor company. Mealtimes were a chore. The only levity was an embarrassed hotel waiter who delivered a bouquet of flowers and a magnum of champagne, proclaiming, 'For the honeymoon couple.' The finance company had had them delivered, but the hotel had confused the sentiment. It raised a brief light-hearted dialogue, but generally the atmosphere was tense.

The few days in New York quickly passed. I spent the evenings in the large hotel bar while Max was happy to stay in the hotel room.

We packed our bags, paid our bills and waited for the coach to take us to JFK airport for the final leg of our adventure. The QE2 had been sumptuous, but the departure lounge for Concorde was something special. Smoked salmon, caviar, finest champagne and cigars. Nothing was spared.

The atmosphere on board was exciting and infectious. The plane itself was narrow: two seats, the aisle, then two more seats. The chairs were leather and very comfortable. The whole experience made you smile with excitement. After take-off there was a buzz in the cabin. Fellow passengers were very chatty and noisy. 'Mach 1,' announced the captain; 'Mach 2,' the screen informed us. Soon we were landing this magnificent beast. Five days to cross to America and four hours to return. It seemed incredible.

Our chauffeur was there to greet us as soon as we were back down to earth on a drizzly M4 motorway. He brought us up to speed on news we had missed and we chatted for most of the journey home. He must have noticed a difference with Max because he commented.

'Oh, just very tired, boyo!' said Max. 'I'll be alright after a good night's sleep in my own bed!'

The chauffeur gave me a sly quizzical look. I passed it off.

I spent the evening answering Sue's many questions. I tried to be as positive about the holiday as possible and luckily she seemed genuinely pleased that I'd had such a good time. I felt very uncomfortable and resolved to try to repair the damage with Max that this trip had created.

After sorting out several issues with Jack, we weren't surprised to find business had been very slow. He had sold three cars, which for the middle of December was very creditable. Slowly I picked up the reins of the business and carried on. Max, however, was in a different place.

On day two of our return I told Max we were closing early; we'd go down the Feathers, a small, discreet hotel on the outskirts of Bradeley, and have a chat. Over drinks Max got serious and informed me that he couldn't get Claudia out of his head. They had been in constant telephone contact and he was going to Chicago with a view to staying. He brought out a photograph of Claudia from his hip pocket to show me.

'Madness,' I said. 'Give it a week and this holiday romance will seem like a wild dream.'

Well, that week came and went. Max was no less useless, like a lovestruck teenager. It was lucky that it was the middle of December with little pre-Christmas business. Max showed Jack and anyone who entered the garage the picture of Claudia; all thought it was funny and harmless.

'He'll come to his senses,' said Jack. 'It's pure fantasy.

He's not going to jeopardise thirty years of married life and a business for a bit of Yankee fluff!'

'I sure hope so,' I said, 'because it'll have to be resolved soon. I can't go on like this!'

Things seemed to settle in the week leading to Christmas and Max seemed more normal. However, on the 22nd of December he hit me with a bombshell.

'Mark,' he announced, 'I've got my tickets for a trip to Chicago, the day after Boxing Day. I'm going and I'm not coming back. Claudia's putting me up and she's going to find me casual work at her travel agency. I want you to buy me out of the business!'

'But, but,' – my mind was racing – 'but what if it doesn't work out, Max?'

'That's my problem, boyo, but don't try to change my mind. It's made up.'

'What about Muriel? Have you told your wife what's going on?'

'Leave Muriel out of this,' said Max angrily. 'That's no concern of yours!'

At that I knew in my heart the Max Value partnership was dead. I couldn't work with the Max who'd just shown his true colours.

'Righto, Max, whatever you want. I'm not going to fight you. Whatever you want is alright with me!' I had decided appeasement might lead to a better working atmosphere.

With this Max seemed to change; he became more reasonable. The old Max emerged, trying to justify his comments and actions. He confided in me that he had not told Muriel, but before he left he would tell her that he was going to look at some American cars for a client of the garage. Whatever happened, he would return and face the music with Muriel and conclude his affairs in the UK.

I decided to seek Sue's advice. When I told her the whole story that evening she was absolutely horror-struck. She was very upset at Max's behaviour on board the cruise liner. This prompted her to declare I should end the partnership forthwith.

'Look after yourself, Mark. Don't worry about Max. He hasn't played fair with you,' kept ringing in my ears.

Max duly acknowledged the end of our partnership. He seemed very amicable and trusting. When I told Jack he didn't seem at all concerned and was quite light-hearted about it all.

'Randy old dog, didn't know he had it in him!' was his comment. 'Far as I'm concerned, good luck to him; you only live once. If he doesn't come back, which he will, you carry on and we'll just keep things as they are!'

I touched on things with Max. He was in another continent, however. 'I'll be back after the New Year and we'll go to the bank and sort out you being sole owner,' he said. Fine by me.

Christmas and Boxing Day came and went, and life without Max had begun when, mid-afternoon, a distraught Muriel phoned. I couldn't understand a word she was saying through the trauma and the tears.

'Sue, get yourself ready, we're going to see Muriel.'

When she opened the door Muriel looked awful. She was pale, tearful and in shock. We sat her down, made a cup of tea and listened to her story.

'What's going on, Mark?' she asked. 'Max has taken every penny out of our bank account.'

'What did he say he was doing, Muriel?' I asked her.

'Oh, he's gone to look at some American cars on business or something. He's been behaving very strangely lately, ever since he came back from that QE2 trip.'

Sue gave me a knowing look.

'Well, brace yourself, Muriel,' I said, and I recounted the whole series of events.

Before we left I phoned Muriel's daughter, who came to comfort her distraught mother.

First thing in the morning I phoned the bank, who informed me Max had in fact written a cheque for £23,727 to himself, with my countersignature, for transfer to an American bank. They were going to seek my verbal approval before releasing the funds. When I informed them that my countersignature was obviously counterfeit, Mr Jackman, my business manager, agreed to stop it. He was obviously concerned that a sum of that size would clear the account. I went to see him, took a photocopy of the cheque for evidence and explained what was happening. He was very fair and helpful and agreed to encash £5,000 and note it. I took the money to Muriel, who hugged me. She was now turning angry at Max's betrayal.

The next week was spent seeing solicitors and bank managers who recorded everything and elevated my position at Max Value Cars to sole proprietor. The partnership was dissolved and Max was history.

The following weeks were spent changing bank accounts and looking after Muriel. She had heard nothing from Max. I took a call when he realised no money was forthcoming from the business.

'But Max, you promised you were coming back to sort out your affairs, face to face!'

'I'm going to have to now,' he snarled, knowing he'd been caught out.

Business carried on as before into January and February. Friends rallied round and helped. Sue took a more active part, doing more administrative work and manning the office and phone. Muriel put her house up for sale and started divorce proceedings. Car sales were steady through an economically tough time. Plenty of people enquired if I needed a partner or an extra pair of hands in sales. I didn't wish to engage anyone just yet, but slowly, throughout the weeks that followed, it became obvious that seven days a week and twelve-hour days would take their toll.

A letter arrived from Chicago. Max had engaged a low-rate solicitor with a claim for his share of the business being $150,000. It upset me, but my solicitor just laughed and stated that any such claims were a costly nonsense for Max because he had no claim unless he served it through a British professional in person: something he didn't seem to want to countenance.

Months went by and Muriel sold her house and moved in with her daughter. Jack was becoming steadily more helpful and called in daily with advice and offers of assistance. The business was still running slowly and steadily. The bank was happy enough during its three-month reviews.

Slowly I had grown less dependent on Jack's supply of vehicles for sale or return. The rates had turned from

65:35% for Jack to 30:70% in my favour. Jack was slowly supplying other garages and my dependency on him was far less, and therefore our relationship was more healthy from my point of view. I had found other sources of supply, i.e. sales managers of main agents, which provided better quality cars at a lower price.

Jack kept hinting about employing a close friend of his to work with me. An interview was arranged. However, I found Alan Dix to be a little too bland. He seemed to have little energy and had hardly set the world on fire at his previous employers. He needed a good shake! I preferred a young friend of Sue's brother who, although totally inexperienced, was a fast learner and bursting with energy and enthusiasm. He was very affable and friendly and would be a hit with the customers.

Jack took the news badly and went off in a huff. Our relationship never recovered. Although he didn't say so, I could tell young Christian was not going to meet with his approval. Slowly I sold Jack's cars and noticed he didn't replace them until, with just six vehicles on site, he announced one morning he would collect them for the site of a competitor. With no hard feelings, but it was time for a change. The relief was palpable and the corner was turned. It was now 100% my business with no interference from Max or Jack.

Chapter 5

The months passed and business was very steady. Young Christian proved to be an absolute godsend. The few mistakes he made were more than made up for by his infectious enthusiasm. The older ladies loved him and he seemed to help sell cars purely by his positive attitude.

Muriel and her relatives were a source of support. At first I had weekly updates and offers of support from her brothers, both financial and by way of physical assistance – driving and helping with domestic duties. Charlie, her eldest brother, was a builder who built a security wall and gate. He wouldn't hear of recompense. Apparently Max and his lady friend had split and Max was returning to the UK with tail suitably between legs.

Almost a year had passed and in late November I was opening the gate to the garage when I noticed a familiar shape skulking by the office.

'Hello, boyo. Got a cup of tea for a thirsty traveller?'

Max looked older and very dishevelled. I should have been angry, but I couldn't help smiling and wanting to hear his story.

'I know, I know, I've been a prize prat,' he said. 'I've lost everything with Muriel. Won't even speak to me.'

'Can you blame her, Max?' I asked. 'You dropped her in a cruel way without a second thought.'

But with that came an almighty crash. It turned out that the hire car Max had collected from Heathrow had rolled backwards, straight into the metal gate port Charlie had erected weeks earlier. Max was used to his American autoboxes and had forgotten to engage the handbrake of his manual.

'Don't need handbrakes on an auto,' he moaned. 'Just look at the damage. Don't suppose you can lend me a car for a few days, Mark?'

He'd lost none of his cheek. I just shook my head and told him Muriel was now co-owner of the garage and to ask her. He didn't look very keen. In the weeks after Max had left, my solicitor had drawn up legal papers transferring Max's share to Muriel, who in turn had transferred the business to my care and supervision.

When I next spoke to Muriel she was incredulous at Max's nerve. David, her other brother, was desperate to find him, but Max had many friends and he sought refuge in his home country of Wales. Over the following years I heard stories of his exploits and, without Muriel to steady him, the last I heard he was homeless, living a squalid existence at a down-and-out's shelter in Swansea.

*

The months rolled by and Christian kept up his good work. During the week I was able to leave him for longer periods. He seemed to relish the challenge and responsibility of it all. I managed the odd day off or day at the auction to buy my own cars. He always seemed to sell a car. If there was a part-exchange he insisted on my final say of price with the customer. He generally drove a harder bargain than I would. Life was pretty steady.

Over this period Susan and I had been mapping out what life should hold due to the success of the business. She had ambitions of her own.

'I've always wanted to run a pub, Mark,' she said time and time again.

Her parents had run a large club affiliated to a leisure complex in Cornwall. Sue grew up in a luxury flat above the club and as a little girl wanted for nothing. She loved the noise and the attention everyone gave her and now hankered after the social aspect of the business.

'But it's hard work and long hours,' I told her. 'Your life is not your own!'

I tried to dissuade her, but secretly I was excited by the prospect of a new challenge. After a long dialogue we agreed it might be just the challenge we both needed. The garage ran itself, ably assisted by Christian, and it had become a steady humdrum existence just keeping all the plates spinning. Operation Pub Find would be a new top priority.

Battan's Weekly had never been so studiously inspected. Every evening we did a 'mystery shop' on pubs dotted around the South West, Wales and the Cotswolds. Most were small, uninspiring run-down establishments. It was no surprise they wanted rid. All the profitable, well-run businesses had full car parks and no prospect of the brewery or business owner wanting to lease or sell.

We had many evenings out but, months later, still no sign of a business. I had put the word out that a 'friend' was looking for a pub business to all my contacts and the Rotary club I had joined, but nothing. Until one rainy Monday morning I had a strange call saying, 'Jim Davis here.'

He explained that he was acting on behalf of his uncle, who, after nearly forty years running the Silversmith's Arms in Bradeley, had had enough and wished to retire. The pub in question was rather old-fashioned but the building was magnificent in its size and history. It was a locals' pub which served excellent food, albeit with a limited menu. Jim's uncle would only lease the pub and eventually sell to someone who would run his business 'properly'. No chains or get-rich-quick merchants – no jukeboxes or plastic fitments. He wanted no truck with anyone who didn't see his rather old-fashioned, traditionalist vision. We agreed to see him that evening.

Three hours of negotiations brought an outline agreement. More importantly, Sid (Jim's uncle) and Sue clicked. Their vision and ideas for the pub dovetailed beautifully and I could see Sid was smitten with Sue's feminine charms, and therefore her ideas of running the pub just as it was were received without question. Sue complimented Sid on every aspect of his pub and after a short while he was putty in her hands. The first three months would be a joint effort and then Sid would hand over total control to Sue. After six months, if both parties agreed, a formal lease agreement would be signed with the option to purchase after twelve months if the business was on a sound financial footing. This really was Sid's baby!

It was hard work for Sue and me. The days, weeks

and months flew by and soon Christmas and New Year came and went. The pub game was lucrative, but you earned every penny. Sid had finally handed over complete control to Sue and he even went days and then weeks before calling in 'just for a quiet pint'. I was so pleased that Sue had her own business and was even enjoying all aspects, including recruitment of staff. I, however, was not so fortunate in this department.

During the seven months Sue had been running the Silversmith's I had noticed the garage's profits were slightly disappointing. Business was slower and units sold and profit margins were dipping. The rest of my trade sources were more than happy with the business and they hadn't noticed a dip. I couldn't put my finger on anything specific, but figures just didn't tally. Christian was not as concerned, and passed off the slowdown in trade as a lack of advertising, but that didn't explain the reduced profit margins. I'd noticed that a lot of deals did not involve part-exchanges, which had been more prevalent in latter years. When I challenged Christian he explained that a lot of people had passed on their old car to family, friends and work colleagues, and had then negotiated a discount for a 'straight sale' – i.e. no part-exchange to dispose of. Something in Christian's body language and a slight colouring of his cheeks made me uncomfortable.

When I discussed this with Sue, she seemed distant. However, next day she hit upon an idea. Why didn't I act unaware, phone some of the customers and ask if we could buy their part-exchange?

'They'll soon tell you whether you didn't offer enough for their car or why they didn't part-exchange it with you! It'll also be good for public relations. It might be boring, Mark, but at least it'll put your mind at rest.'

I decided that I'd pop into the garage in the early evening and phone some of the customers from the latest sales; it'd be good PR. The garage closed at 6pm, so I called round at 6.30. I wondered whose Volvo estate was parked over the road, and then I caught sight of two men sitting in the front seats. One was Jack and the other was Christian. They looked very furtive and serious. I was sure they caught my sight before Jack sped off like a bat out of hell. My heart was thumping and the blood was burning into my face. My mind was racing with a myriad of thoughts, but mostly I felt empty and disgusted.

The first phone call with shaking hands unravelled the truth. Mr Palmer explained that he had part-exchanged his Talbot Horizon that he'd had from nearly new. He was puzzled by why it didn't appear on his invoice but assumed that was how we did our paperwork. Four more phone calls untangled a further three part-exchanges not declared on our records. I didn't sleep a wink that night!

Christian appeared at 9.30 that following morning. To say he looked nervous would be an understatement. He looked like the condemned man that he was.

'My office – now,' I thundered, surprising myself with the strength of my anger. 'You'd better explain yourself before the police arrive!'

His face was ashen. He stuttered a garbled, rehearsed explanation that was an obvious pack of lies. Eventually, after he'd broken down, he made some sense. Apparently Jack had cajoled and forced Christian into his fraud. As an older and more experienced man he'd convinced Christian he was worth more financially than I was paying him. His responsibility and level of business were worth more. If he sold the part-exchanges to Jack, Christian would be rewarded handsomely, in keeping with his new elevated role.

I explained to Christian that he'd been used by Jack to even a score which was in Jack's imagination. He would not gain financially because he would lose any salary now due. The loss of his job and reputation in Bradeley would be a massive blow to Christian, but the trust was now gone.

'Now get out of my garage before the police arrive and before I press charges against you and Jack!'

He sidled away with a look of deep sorrow and remorse. A look that told me he was truly sorry, and one that conveyed the enormity of what he'd done. Christian wasn't the real villain; that was Jack. I needed to exact revenge.

This experience taught me one valuable lesson. Like the matriarchal mama in a Greek restaurant, always have your hands on the till. Never neglect your business or trust anyone outside the family. 'If they can steal from you, they will' was my new opinion.

As for Jack, I spread the story around the motor business community of Bradeley. Many hard-bitten motor traders weren't shocked and it was the slow death knell of Jack's business. Once he'd lost their trust he lost their business, and eighteen months later he'd sold up and retired. He bought a villa in Cyprus and watched the fishing boats. I heard that the Cypriot government confiscated his property. An expatriate

Greek Cypriot was reinstated into his family property, and this was upheld by the courts. Jack was spending vast amounts in the courts to fight this, but it seemed the Greek Cypriot had the original genuine deeds of the land and buildings. Oh dear, I felt so sorry for Jack!

*

Life in the next few months was hectic, but running the garage was enjoyable. I'd forgotten how much I'd missed the daily routine of the motor trade. Life was tiring. A call came out of the blue.

'It's me, Mark. I need a favour.'

The voice was that of Robbie. He went on to explain that he'd worked at the local Volvo garage for the last two years. He was still with Lauren and had settled down. However, three months ago a new manager had arrived who was not enamoured with Robbie's casual approach to life. He'd baited Robbie from day one until finally one Monday afternoon Robbie had seen red, told the manager what he thought of the new sales systems, questioned the manager's parentage and walked out.

'The key for my Volvo estate ended up down the drain, so I literally walked home,' he said. 'Please can I give you a hand, Mark? I don't want any money. If Lauren thinks I'm not working I'm a dead man.'

'Of course you can, Robbie,' I heard myself saying. 'I'll pay you commission when you sell anything and you can call round and pick up a car.'

The next six months were the best for business and fun since we'd opened. Robbie was a bundle of energy and fresh air. We sparked off each other and the atmosphere in the garage was electric. There was a friendly rivalry between us over who would sell the most. No cause was lost and any customer who walked on to the forecourt had no excuse but to buy a car. Sue even complained about the length of time I was spending at the garage. Profits were brilliant, but the pace and workload were enormous.

The following six months were spent in a daze of activity. As our reputation grew, so did sales. People were recommending family members who bought on trust. To combat the stress Robbie and I were spending more time in Sue's pub. She gave us the odd cold glance, but I satisfied myself with the thought that at least we were increasing Sue's takings.

This nightly routine was becoming too regular. My daily hangovers and Sue's nagging eventually hit home.

'It's too easy, Robbie. We've got to cut back,' I said.

The look on his face told me Lauren had already broached the subject.

'Yeah, I'm getting grief at home,' he said. 'Still, it was good while it lasted.'

We spent the next few months like the professional business people we'd become, home on time and destressed. I mooted the possibility of expanding the empire to Robbie; we could look for another site. I was mindful of any trust issues, but Robbie had proved in the last year that he was a trustworthy colleague and employee.

There were two or three possible sites, but they were just too far from Bradeley's town centre. One was near a new housing development but on a busy, fast road. Another was tucked away from the known 'car alley' and would take a lot of advertising. I'd used my time to prospect potential car sales sites, checking with local people and estate agents, but it proved a frustrating and time-consuming exercise. I'd called at the Silversmith's unexpectedly to surprise Sue on more than one occasion, only finding a flustered Eunice coping with the busy lunchtime trade.

'She's at the cash-and-carry, Mark,' seemed to be her usual line. 'Any message?'

'No, no,' I replied. 'I'll see her later.'

Eventually a possible site did result. A small engineering company called Campbell's on a busy main road into Bradeley had closed several years previously. The site was nearly derelict and it had been vandalised and used as a shelter for street people. The council had compulsorily purchased the property with a view to demolition and road widening. Sean Grebble rang from Nash & Co., a local commercial agent, with the news that because of spending cuts the local authority had frozen all road developments and were therefore willing to sell the whole site.

'It's a steal at £175,000 for a quarter-acre prime site, Mark. It won't be long before the developers snap it up!'

Mr Grebble didn't know that, through my contacts in the council via Rotary, I knew the council wouldn't sell to any known developers. The property was to be sold only to a local established business and it could be purchased for nearer £125,000, which was their bottom line.

Robbie and I furtively examined the potential. The traffic past the site was slow-moving due to two sequences of traffic lights. Access and road prominence were excellent. The buildings and open parking area would lend themselves perfectly to offices, workshops and an open display area for approximately fifty cars. Building work would be mainly for a garage and paint shop, but the main structure of the existing engineering workshop could easily be adapted. The existing offices could be used with some cosmetic work. There was even a windowed area which could be adapted to accommodate a three-vehicle showroom.

'Wow, what an opportunity, Mark,' gushed Robbie. 'The potential is massive!'

'Yeah, but so's the cost, and where's the gold money pot to pay for it all?' I asked, trying to curb the adrenaline already pumping through my veins.

'That's for Archie to sort.' He meant Mr Archibald, my business manager at Midshires Bank.

Sue seemed lukewarm when I broached the idea of expanding the car business. She seemed to think we had plenty with the lease of the pub and car lot.

'But that's why, if we can purchase this site, it's our pension for the future,' I said. 'We can work for another twenty years or so and then retire young enough to enjoy it all comfortably.'

'You do what you like. You will anyway,' she retorted sourly.

This was out of character for Sue, who always talked through her opinion and was usually right.

My meeting with Mr Archibald couldn't have been timed better. He had just returned from a three-day bank seminar aimed at expanding local businesses and improving the bank's presence within the Bradeley area. More support and time was to be given locally and sensible, viable business expansion programmes were to be encouraged. He knew the site in question as Midshires had been Campbell's bankers throughout.

'A good company, well run. Just couldn't compete with the Far East, lower wage costs and dwindling profits. Sad, same old story of manufacturing in this country,' was how Mr Archibald summed it up. 'Still – every cloud. Now, let's have a look at your figures, Mr Leigh.'

After crunching some forecasts and analysis from my accounts of Max and the early days up to the present day, Mr Archibald seemed moderately impressed. He was lukewarm on the pub's turnover and profit ratios but understood that it was a stand-alone business, not to be included with this current proposal. Mr Archibald concluded that the car lot would have to be secured against any borrowings for the Campbell site mortgage redevelopment.

'Because your car lot is leased, Midshires will also require another form of collateral, normally a second charge against your private dwelling,' he said seriously.

'Oh, I was hoping that we could avoid that,' I muttered.

'Hmm, I'll see what I can do, Mark, but due to your limited years in business and short business history, it may not be my decision,' he said.

To say that Sue was angry when I related the events of the day would be a monumental understatement. She hit the roof.

'Over my dead body will any bank have a charge on *my* home. I will not sign any such agreement. My name is on the deeds too, Mark,' she spat. 'Just forget the whole thing. They will provide the mortgage on the building, there's plenty of equity in bricks and mortar, why do they need *our* bricks and mortar?'

She had a point. I'd never seen Sue so stressed and angry. There was a mistrust and coldness in her voice that was not like her. I wondered if worries at the pub were biting at her.

'Tell you what,' I heard myself saying, 'next week is quiet, just before Easter. Let's have a few days away. The change of air will do us both good!'

Normally she would jump at the chance of a short break, but this offer did little to change her black mood and she stormed away, shouting that she had too much work to do at the pub and couldn't just go swanning off when the mood took her.

As events unfolded, the need for further sureties and safeguards did not materialise. My solicitor Mr Herbert rang Mr Archibald and reminded him that all personal and business accounts were with the Midshires bank. Therefore, any problems that might occur could be underpinned by 'set-off'. This apparently is legalised daylight robbery from one account to another if you have more than one account. The value of stock and the positive assets in the car lot more than superseded any loan or mortgage required for the new venture. The bank had their belt and braces and umbrella in case of a rainy day.

This did not, however, ease the rumblings in my gut about Sue. She was increasingly short-tempered and irritable. Any of my inferences on this theme were met with arguments and denials. Something was wrong and I needed to find out what it was. I decided to pay her more attention, which meant spending more time at the Silversmith's.

'Did I ever tell you about my time on the Kenyan railways, Mark?'

It was a question posed almost every time I encountered Len 'Lenny' Johanson. He was a tall South African with an engaging smile and a big personality. Scotch was his drink and storytelling was his forte. He kept the regulars engaged for hours with stories from the bush of safaris, railways, gold and diamond smugglers, and the corrupt activities of the many African bureaucrats he had encountered over the years. He lived with his sister and brother-in-law in Bradeley, after escaping Mugabe's regime in Zimbabwe. Lenny worked part-time for the local tourist information centre and was busy writing his book. 'It's all in the book, Mark!' was his usual reply if you needed to hear the conclusion of his meandering tales. The offer of another tot in his special cut crystal whisky glass usually did the trick.

Trade and takings at the pub were encouraging. It was a steady, solid business. An all-year-round reliable, plodding venture. Food sales had dropped slightly with the opening of a fast-food venture opposite, but our chef Lionel had updated his menu and improved the lunchtime snacks, which increased sales, and by and large everything seemed on an even keel. The staff all knew their jobs and Sue had everything under control. There seemed to be no problems with the customers or the general running of day-to-day activities. The profits were fair, there were no money problems and all the staff seemed content. Perhaps I was imagining things!

As the weeks passed business was brisk. The pub and car lot ran themselves, and a mortgage and loan to develop Campbell's had been approved. Work had started on a full workshop and site refurbishment. The atmosphere at home, however, was not so dynamic. In fact it was decidedly frosty. Sue wouldn't talk and was civil but aloof. She was very vague and distant. She lived at the Silversmith's and returned very late and sometimes, at weekends, not at all, texting that she would stay over for an early start at the accounts, restocking, order taking and so on. Something was very wrong. I caught a glimpse of some pills at the top of her handbag. Valium. No more than four to be taken daily, prescribed by our family doctor at the Bradeley Health Centre.

I needed to discover what was happening to Sue. She wouldn't talk, so I had to use devious methods to satisfy myself.

'Robbie, I need to borrow your car for a couple of days. Don't ask me why, and you'll be in sole charge. I'll ring you if I need anything, but trust me, it's important!'

'Sure, Mark, take all the time you need.' He could tell by my face it was important. I'm sure he had plenty of questions, but he was diplomatic enough not to venture.

'Oh, and I'd be grateful if this is just between us.'

'Sure, no problem,' he replied.

It was nothing like the detective stories on television. In reality, following somebody in a stake-out situation was just plain boring. I shadowed Sue for forty-eight hours non-stop. I sat outside the pub across the road and watched until she took a direct line straight home, to the cash-and-carry, the hairdresser's, the bank, the post office and so on. For those two days all I found out was that a detective's job is just plain cold and boringly monotonous.

On day three I was pleased to report back to Robbie and the world of motor car trivia. Once he'd briefed me on events and I'd returned urgent calls, I called on the work in progress at Campbell's. Things were running well and Ernie, the site foreman, was unusually upbeat about the work.

'Another few weeks and she'll be ready, Mr Leigh,' he said.

Well, at least work life was going well, I thought.

Those weeks flew by and it was time to buy office furniture and stationery for the new site.

'Come on, Robbie, just close up for a couple of hours. Two heads are better than one and you've got a good eye for a bargain. We'll try that warehouse off the high street that sells second-hand desks and chairs.'

We parked up and although it was mid-October there was an icy nip in the air. The mood turned icier still when I literally bumped into a brassy creature dressed in fake tiger skin and cheap scent, with frizzy bleached hair. Bangles and an orange tan completed the look.

'Keep your missus away from my Len, mate,' she spat. 'I suppose she's told you what's going on. My Len, being tempted by the likes of that?'

With that she was gone.

The next two hours were a blur. Robbie looked concerned – I just looked stupefied. We abandoned the search for furniture and Robbie drove us back to his flat, where he poured me a stiff brandy. For the next few hours he listened whilst I poured out my thoughts and fears.

'But she's just a vindictive old tart trying to cause trouble. Your missus wouldn't give that Len house room,' said Robbie.

But I knew from the look in that woman's eyes that there was something in the story.

Robbie was looking at everything in a logical way. 'Why would she jeopardise all you two have got together?' he asked, which struck a chord. Why indeed? There was only one way to find out.

'Robbie, lock up the garage, will you? I'm going to the Silversmith's!'

A kind of serenity and placid calm overwhelmed me. I told myself to be totally rational and not to lose it. 'Just act normally,' I whispered to myself.

Sue was busying herself with brewery orders but eventually she came over for a coffee. I relayed the story as calmly and naturally as I could manage. The colour drained from Sue's face but, of course, she stammered an almost believable explanation that this 'Maureen' woman was Len's fancy piece, who had an incredibly jealous nature. She'd accused every female member of staff in the pub and was so venomous that Sue had barred her, resulting in the unpleasant scene in Bradeley. However, something in Sue's reaction warned my instincts that all was far from well.

Robbie was almost jubilant. 'See – I knew there'd be nothing in it, Mark.'

Just some crazy hag causing trouble because she was barred. I decided, now that Sue knew she was under scrutiny, to watch the developments.

The next few months were incredibly busy. The opening of the new garage was taking an age to finalise. Sue's attitude changed almost completely. She was cheerful and friendly. Very polite and caring, and almost back to the old Sue, but something was missing.

The opening of the garage was a blur of activity, stress and phone calls. The *Bradeley Echo* had done a full-page feature with accompanying adverts from all our suppliers and supporters. Robbie was inspirational with his efforts and support, and family members all helped. An open day and evening with bouncy castle, refreshments, a barbershop singing group and a juggler and magician entertained. People were milling around and a carnival atmosphere enabled everyone to have a fun day.

At 11pm the last family member had gone and Robbie and I toasted a great success.

'That's how to open a garage,' he said.

'You've been great, mate,' I said. 'I couldn't have done any of this without you.'

'Agh, go on, get off home, Sue'll think you've got a fancy woman too,' he blurted out before he thought of how cutting that sounded. I could see by Robbie's face he realised he'd overstepped.

'Good, might make her realise what she's been missing,' I lied to make Robbie feel better.

The house was incredibly quiet. I thought Sue must have retired to bed, but there was no sign. Must have gone back to the pub, I thought, but a horrible black feeling of gloom engulfed me. Her phone went straight to the answering machine.

When I awoke next morning there was still no sign of

her, either at home or at the Silversmith's. The staff at the pub looked sheepish and wouldn't meet my eyes. I was getting worried for her safety. Still, there were two garages to run and Robbie needed help.

However, for some unknown reason I was drawn to another part of Bradeley which was purely residential. This new housing development was part of a housing association and council initiative to establish affordable housing for young families and local people, built on the site of a large Victorian workhouse and lunatic asylum. The main hospital building had been retained and converted into modern flats; the acres of recuperative gardens were now little boxes of starter homes and terraced modern town houses. As I drove down one of these undistinguished streets I spotted Sue's car parked in a drive.

I hammered on the door. I don't know who was more surprised when the front door opened. Sue's face was a picture of horror. In the background, stumbling around in the hall, was a man's figure.

'Who's there, Sue?'

The unmistakeable voice of Len echoed through. I was so dumbfounded I just turned and told her, 'You deserve each other – good luck!'

'It's not what you think,' was all she could stutter.

Apparently they'd been carrying on for months. All the staff at the Silversmith's knew. Len and Sue had jointly purchased one of the starter terraced houses from the developers through their easy option to buy scheme. Quite when she was going to inform her husband, friends and family was debatable.

The feeling of betrayal and sick, treacherous disgust

began to fill my soul as the weeks passed. I informed my solicitor, who began the painstaking task of sorting out our affairs.

The following weeks were a blur. Disappointment turned to anger. Friends rallied round. Work helped and I threw myself into building up the new garage. Robbie was a real friend. Slowly my mind changed. I mistrusted everyone and bitterness and resentment took over. I instructed my solicitor to sign everything of the Silversmith's over to Sue. I wanted nothing from that business and did not wish to see any staff or customers at any time. Contact with Sue was conducted through my solicitor and luckily no children were involved.

I'd spent three uncomfortable weeks in our house. Luckily it was very sellable and soon the estate agent was calling with an offer. I've since learnt in life that when you're down everyone tries to kick you.

'They're cash buyers, Mark,' said Mr Anthony from Palmerstones Estate Agents, 'but their limit is £5,000 less than you're asking. They've found some evidence of woodworm in the roof timbers and their furniture is mostly wooden.'

'Mr Anthony, four years ago that house was magnificent, now it's infested with woodworm. You earn your commission and tell them I'll treat the beams rather than lower the price.'

My time dealing with 'try-on Charlies' had taught me some lessons. I was short with the estate agent only because he considered my position to be weak and thought I would be desperate for a sale. He was being lazy and not acting with my best interests at heart.

Lo and behold, twenty-four hours later Mr Anthony came back with 'better news'. 'I've managed to persuade them up, but they're still £2,000 short of the asking price, Mark. Can we help in any way?'

This last sentence spurred me to retaliate.

'Yes we can, Mr Anthony. Your company can lower its commission by £1,000 and I will match that, therefore the goal of a £2,000 saving for the buyers will be achieved.'

After a long silence, a lot of spluttering and stammering seemed to cause chaos in Mr Anthony's brain. I was enjoying this and quietly chuckled to myself for the first time in a week.

During a quiet evening staring blankly at the television, I groaned when the doorbell rang. I could distinguish two shadowy figures outside. On opening the door, I found a young couple looking pensive and nervous.

'I hope you don't mind,' the young lad said, 'but Evie and I saw the For Sale sign. I know it's late and we don't have an appointment . . .'

'You want to look round when the house is a mess?' I asked.

'Oh, no,' said the girl, 'I told you to ring the agent. We're so sorr—'

'Don't be daft, but I wasn't kidding about the mess. Come in.'

For two hours this young couple charmed me with their natural honesty and enthusiasm. Apparently John's parents had lived on this street twenty years ago and they loved the area. John had spent his childhood around and about and they would love to return. They had recently married, had good jobs and a mortgage in place and had family help with a deposit. I explained the position of the offer and told them if they paid the full asking price and saw Mr Anthony the next morning I would favour their presence in the house.

Next day Mr Anthony was totally shocked by events. He started to inform me that he couldn't have two offers. It was all most irregular and he couldn't do business in this unorthodox fashion.

'Fine,' I said, 'you either sell my house to John and Evie or take your board out of my garden. Send them to see me and I'll do the deal without an estate agent's assistance.' I reminded him that I'd sold the house myself at the full asking price and he had wanted a £5,000 reduction and his commission.

Sorting out a deal with my young couple was incredibly easy. Palmerstones tried to bully them into a mortgage at a higher rate with a company they weren't comfortable with. I phoned them and invited them round in the evening. I explained everything and told them they would be the new owners. They were to get their finances in order and wait for a good friend of mine, a conveyancing solicitor, to be in touch. 'If Palmerstones get heavy, refer them to me; don't be bullied. Just remember you're not a client of Palmerstones – you didn't contact them before and ask for details of the property.' All of which was true.

Within a month John and Evie moved into the house. Palmerstones threatened to sue me for breach of contract. They sent an invoice to my solicitor and me for commission on the house sale. I in turn re-invoiced them for an equal amount for removal of a redundant

For Sale board which was illegally parked in my garden. Jocelyn, my solicitor, was the talk of the Round Table with his defiant stance against Palmerstones, who were seen in Bradeley as rather pompous.

'It's time someone pricked their giant ego,' said Jocelyn over drinks. 'They won't take it any further, and if they do we'll just let everyone know about their lazy sales methods.'

That last sentence got me thinking.

I spoke to Robbie about his future.

'How would you like to be a partner in this garage business?'

He seemed dumbfounded. He had nothing financial to offer.

'You've got better than money; you've got yourself and the future,' I said. 'Obviously I'd be senior partner, but, if you run the garage businesses with help, you'll have a salary and a share of the profits.'

I meanwhile had a germ of an idea for a different business direction.

Bradeley had expanded over the last fifteen years with two large housing estates, which were Moogley Fields and Barderley, growing from tiny villages into suburban sprawls. RAF land had been sold to large developers who had turned these green fields into rows of terraced boxes and starter houses for the masses. They weren't pretty, but they fulfilled a need. There would be another 2,000 new homes built in addition to the 3,000-plus already in existence.

My encounter with Palmerstones had convinced me that the estate agents of Bradeley were elitist and dictatorial. They were old school tie and reluctant to change. They operated in much the same way as they had for decades, and only in their town centre locations. They ran a cartel of a fixed commission of 2.5% of the selling price and did little for their fee. They did not accompany the prospective buyers, so in effect you paid them for selling your own house! If the buyer wanted any assistance with a mortgage they were a nuisance. 'Go and see your bank manager for money!' was the usual response; a back-scratching arrangement with an old school pal or Round Table colleague was the most effort these agents seemed to offer. Descriptions of the properties and specifications seemed a work of fiction.

Chapter 6

I met Jocelyn at the Feathers and put my ideas to him. When he digested them he seemed slightly bewildered.

'It's either a brilliant idea or it'll fall flat in six months.'

I'd just spent an hour explaining that the estate agency business needed a complete, radical new approach. Put an agency in the shopping areas of both Moogley Fields and Barderley, where the houses were being sold. Offer a complete service with accompanied viewings and polite, young, eager salespeople to answer any questions on the local area. Offer a mortgage, insurance and removal service within the branch and take a commission. In fact make it a one-stop shop with the services of a conveyancer.

Jocelyn put up some objections, but I countered every one and eventually he could see that, although untried, there was no reason a local suburban estate agent working on a lower fixed fee for a house sale could not work. The overheads would be lower and even at half the price of conventional estate agents there was still a superb profit to be made. Jocelyn must have been impressed because he insisted on a 50:50 partnership which included his lucrative conveyancing profits. We were in the estate agency business!

An empty shop unit next to the dry cleaner and fish and chip shop in the shopping area of Moogley Fields seemed a modest place to start a new venture. However, the rent and rates were equally modest and refurbishment costs would be little. A cab firm had been the last tenant, so desks and an open-plan layout were already in place.

The locals took a little time to understand the simplicity of our business plan. We took out two-page spreads in the *Bradeley Echo* on the Thursday property page slot. I distributed leaflets by hand throughout Moogley Fields. Slowly but steadily enquiries by phone started to come in. Most people couldn't believe their luck. They were pleasantly surprised by the simplicity and low commission price all-in package. I lied through my teeth and said twenty-four houses were on our books, but as soon as the first customer placed their property and trust with us, the business took off.

I employed Sally, who had been a brilliant admin girl at Spearlings. She was looking for part-time work after her little girl had started school. She was excellent with people and a camera. Soon our window was full of pictures of houses for sale.

I knew after two weeks the Leigh and St John estate agency was a brilliant idea. Jocelyn couldn't have been more pleased or more busy. He took an office at the site in Moogley Fields and juggled his day between two businesses.

We knew the business was popular with customers and professionals alike. Every day we had calls from surveyors, mortgage brokers and even rival 'out of town' estate agents all wanting to be part of our success. Jocelyn fielded the surveyors and the finance boys. I spoke to the rivals who wanted to repeat our formula in their town.

Sally and I were rushed off our feet and soon we had eighty-seven properties on our books. We realised we were on to something with enormous potential but needed assistance. Jocelyn was brilliant – his revenue from the conveyancing work kept us afloat in the early months. We soon realised we needed more experienced staff. Jocelyn's knowledge of the business and his contacts enabled us to recruit key people who loved the energy and fresh approach of our new venture.

Soon we had found another office in Barderley; again it was in a small cul-de-sac of retail units, this one next to a funeral director and newsagent. We collected the keys and a fortnight later, with two young staff poached from Palmerstones, we were up and running.

Jocelyn called me into his office one Monday morning.

'What's this?' I asked.

'This' turned out to be franchise agreements for any enterprising speculators who wanted a part of this business.

'Mark, go and see those people who phoned in the first week of trading – with your enthusiasm and sales patter we can have the name of Leigh and St John in every town and city suburb in the South West. We take a percentage of profits and a franchise fee and sit back and let others do the work. They will love the successful formula and will work twice as hard as salaried staff to grow their business. We can still take a commission from any professionals we appoint for them and we'll help with their recruitments.'

Twelve-hour days soon stretched to eighteen, but slowly the offices began to run themselves and Jocelyn and I eased down and watched the cash roll in.

Robbie had mixed fortunes with staff but proved a capable businessman.

'Thirty-two people I've sacked, Mark, according to the accountants!'

I wasn't proud of it, but we now had a great settled team who all knew what was expected. The books of the two garages looked healthy and business was steady if unspectacular. The atmosphere in the two Max Value car showrooms was friendly and cheerful, and my – how time had flown.

Nearly two years had elapsed since I'd last seen Susan. Snippets of gossip had reached me, saying that Len and Sue had lasted less than six months. Sue had grown tired of Len's idle ways, and the tall stories and lies had counteracted the original bonhomie. She'd barred him from the Silversmith's after one too many booze-fuelled arguments and soon his bags were packed and he was jettisoned back to his sister's. The Silversmith's was slowly coming to look very seedy and run-down. The locals were still loyal but the young vibrant spenders were frequenting a new 'state-of-the-art' superpub, built by a large brewery chain on the other side of Bradeley. Sue didn't have the reserves to compete or to improve the pub, so a slow downward spiral would ensue.

*

One Saturday in autumn I was assisting Robbie. He had launched a 'weekend sale' and needed hands on deck. Surprisingly the morning had been quite quiet.

'Calm before the storm, Mark, you'll see,' he retorted when I asked if the road to the garage was closed. Just at this point I looked up to see a face not seen in fifteen years.

'Carol Griffiths, is that you?'

'Carol Potter now, Mark!' she managed to say before I gave her the biggest hug possible and lifted her off the ground.

'Steady, tiger,' she said with the biggest beam on her face.

The next two hours flew by catching up in my office. We'd been inseparable at senior school. She'd married Alan Potter three years after leaving school. I'd broken her heart after some silly row because in those days I'd put sport before girls. I never forgot Carol, but when I heard she'd married and had two boys, well, Susan came along and life took a different path.

'Yes, I know I should have made up with you, Mark, but I was stubborn. Alan was like a lap dog to me; after a few years he bored me stiff. Life was just too cosy and one day I just woke up and decided life was too short for a humdrum existence.'

It seemed she'd found a place to rent, educated the boys and embarked on plenty of adventures including marathons, cycle treks across America and paragliding.

'Phew, you tire me out just talking about your exploits, but why are you looking around my garage?'

She was looking out for a cheap runabout for a work colleague who was wary of salesmen.

'Just look at this Fiesta.'

It'd been an old boy's pride and joy; his eyesight meant he had to relinquish his driving, so he wanted 'Betsy' to go to a good home. Two hours later and the deal was done. Julie, Carol's boss at a local florist, was overjoyed and went off to buy new mats and car seat covers for her new acquisition.

Two nights later, during a strange dream, I woke with a start. That morning I knew I had to phone or see Carol.

'What's Carol's number, Julie? She left her sunglasses in my office,' I lied.

Julie reluctantly obliged me. After an age a gruff male voice answered.

'Mum's gone to Jamaica on holiday.'

'Oh, okay, it'll keep. When's she back?'

'Dunno – about a week,' was the bored response.

Life gathered pace. Seventeen franchises in the South West had been granted in the last five months. Each of them needed visiting and advice, and mentoring was exhausting work. Seven weeks flew by, but one single thought was on my mind.

'Carol, is that you?'

The phone crackled and sounded faint. 'Well, it was this morning, according to the water board. Why? Who's that?'

I'd phoned to explain that I had a £25 intro for her bringing Julie into Max Value's used car sales. She wouldn't hear of taking anything, but I heard myself saying, 'Well, you'll just have to have the reward by way of a meal out for two, including moi, at a restaurant of your choice! It's this Thursday, at eight sharp.'

Carol looked lovely, with her Caribbean tan. The warm late summer evening meant that it kept light until 10pm. I had not been this nervous in years. Any business deal or bank manager was a cakewalk compared to being cool in Carol's company. After a couple of hours and some drinks I began to relax slightly, but, although the food was delicious, I was too nervous to eat much. I dropped Carol off at her home and felt like an awkward schoolboy when I stammered, 'That was a lovely evening. I'll call you to do it again sometime!'

Carol managed, 'Yes, please do, Mark,' with a look on her face which told me she meant what she said.

The following weeks were a whirl. Life had never been so exciting and challenging. Trying to juggle two businesses and seeing Carol was hectic but so rewarding. I'd forgotten what a wonderful person she was. Everyone loved her and her boys were very protective. Although they had friends and girlfriends of their own, they quizzed her on every aspect of her new life, but they could see she was happy.

Jocelyn showed me the figures for the first year's trading, a very healthy profit and a winning formula. Some of the high street agents were trying to hit back. One had launched a similar format, with a fixed-price commission package. However, they had not relocated from Bradeley High Street to the local suburb, for the local market. All they had succeeded in doing was reducing their profits on their traditional sales. So, months later, they abandoned their venture and reverted to their traditional business.

Sales in Moogley Fields and Barderley were

booming, so much so that when two local independent companies followed our lead, I was quite relieved. We couldn't keep that pace up in a growing market and competition for our young staff was healthy.

The franchises were proving to be an inspired decision of Jocelyn's. They accounted for approximately 70% of our revenue. As he said, 'Just sit back and watch the licence fee money swell your retirement pot, Mark!'

Robbie kept me informed on a daily basis of the figures on the two Max Value sites. He'd had issues with staff in our original garage; finding good, honest salespeople was difficult. Many youngsters seemed to think the world owed them a living.

'They don't want to work, Mark, especially at weekends! All they want is to swan around in a flash motor, wear a suit and impress the girls. They think selling is money for old rope!'

'Yeah, just like you at that age, Robbie,' I retorted.

Even he saw the irony of his words. However, I was impressed with his transformation; he was running the two sites efficiently and well. He had taken to management brilliantly, much better than I could have hoped or expected. He earned every penny of the yearly bonus I presented to him. Robbie was so grateful for his opportunity he outlined some of the improvements and plans ahead for the coming years.

Carol couldn't have been more enthusiastic and supportive of the estate agent phenomenon. She understood my worries but her clear, logical thought process calmed any nagging doubts about the speed of growth we were experiencing. My outlook on life and general sense of wellbeing were in sharp contrast to the nightly 'doom and gloom' broadcast by the media.

'Talk about making you feel miserable. They should rename it Bad News at Nine!' commented Carol. 'I'm sure if that newscaster announced anything positive his face would crack.'

'I'll say something positive: why don't we book a holiday? I've always wanted to visit Italy and I haven't had a real break in four years.'

So the two of us checked out the travel agents. Carol was an enthusiastic traveller and soon a package to the Neapolitan Riviera was booked, all four-star and expensive.

'It's all well and good you earning all this money, Mark, but you need to enjoy it, recharge your batteries and see the world.'

I didn't argue.

Whilst on our holiday, I realised what a beautiful person Carol was. She befriended everyone; all the hotel staff were soon smiling and calling to Madam Carol. Her enthusiasm for everything was infectious. One night I mooted the idea of her helping in the estate agency empire, but she showed a side of her character that seemed odd.

'What if I let you down, Mark? I've never done selling and I couldn't lie to anyone.'

'Selling isn't about lying!' I snapped. 'You'd be perfect as you are. "Tell the truth and shame the devil" was invented for sincere business people.'

She looked genuinely shocked and agreed to help in the Barderley office one Saturday to see.

The holiday was wonderful. Trips to Rome and Capri

interrupted lazy days, and soon we returned to the grey, wet tarmac that was Gatwick airport.

Robbie and Jocelyn soon brought me back to speed on that Thursday morning. Max Value had suffered a break-in on the day of departure. Luckily Robbie had not informed me before take-off.

'No point you worrying and spoiling your holiday, Mark,' he said. 'It's all sorted now and the scumbag who stole the radios is banged up.'

Jocelyn was concerned that our Barderley office was underperforming, but everything else was well on track.

'Get yourself a holiday, Jocelyn; it'll do you a world of good.'

Trying to persuade Jocelyn not to work was almost impossible. He worked sixteen-hour days and had no other interests outside of his business life. 'Yeah, let's just get another twelve months' business under our belts and I might look at it.'

I gave him a knowing look.

Carol completed her first Saturday in the estate agency business. She seemed bemused.

'Get your coat,' I said, 'we're going to the Feathers for a bite to eat.'

Over garlic mushrooms she expressed her opinions of her first day.

'All the staff are lovely, Mark,' she said, 'but I'm not so sure about Steve.' Steve Finley was the branch manager and an ex-Palmerstones employee. 'There's nothing I can put my finger on, but there's something about him that doesn't add up.'

'Oh, in what way, Carol?'

'Well, as we were locking up I caught sight of half a dozen toilet rolls under his coat. He was pinching them to take home.'

'Right – anything else?' I asked.

'Yes, he speaks to Hilary as if she's dirt!' Hilary was the office junior just recruited from university after gaining a business degree. 'She doesn't say anything, but I can see she's upset. And he's smarmy with customers, all smiling tiger grin but mumbling when they don't play ball.'

'Okay, Carol, thanks for that.'

I relayed her suspicions to Jocelyn.

'Hmm,' he mused. 'Best I call Mr Rockey to do a bit of digging.'

Mr Rockey was a private detective who had done a lot of work for Jocelyn's solicitor friends. His methods were unorthodox, with lots of hidden cameras and microphones.

'What will he do, Jocelyn?'

'Best you leave that to me. We'll only need a week and then you can see the evidence for yourself!'

*

Steve's face turned grey. Our private viewing, after hours in the Barderley office, would have frightened the toughest of nuts, without Mr Rockey staring intently at him throughout. Stealing from the petty cash box every evening, shouting insults at Hilary, being rude to customers was minor. What upset Jocelyn and me the most were the daily bulletins to the MD at Palmerstones.

'Well, you'd better move, Steve, because when I've finished spreading this news through Bradeley's business community you won't get a job as a paper boy, never mind in management. Now get out!'

Mr Hamley proved a godsend. He was an old acquaintance of Jocelyn. A bachelor, he had decided to retire in his late fifties and regretted it from day one. Long days on his own had him climbing the walls of his luxury bachelor residence. He jumped at our offer and took to the new estate agency format naturally. Thirty-plus years in estate agency gave him just the steady hand needed on this particular wheel. He was popular with staff and customers alike. They loved his easy manner and sense of humour. We loved his stories and reminiscences of his early years working in Muffleyford.

He built up the Barderley branch to be the jewel in the crown. Older clients and first-time buyers enjoyed the atmosphere in the place. Soon the compliments board set up by Mr Hamley was full of goodwill messages. People appreciated his patience and unhurried attention to detail. They sent their friends, neighbours and families in to buy and sell their properties. The local radio station produced a piece on how popular this estate agency had become. The local news team did a five-minute spot on the regional news which was to change our lives completely.

Jocelyn and I were shocked by a telephone call received by Jocelyn one sunny Sunday morning. It came from a stockbroker pal and was rather like a fencing match, but played verbally, not physically.

'How would you react if a client of mine was to show an interest in your estate agency venture, old boy?' was the opening thrust.

'*Not* interested!' was Jocelyn's well-rehearsed riposte.

'Now, now, you've not heard who and why. My client may be interested in your little family venture!'

Apparently no less a figure than Charles Callaghan wanted us to spread our estate agency and allied financial services package throughout Europe and beyond. Charles Callaghan was a massive figure in the world of finance and financial products. He wanted our business to be the McDonald's of estate agency, franchised under a corporate logo. We would head up the company and enjoy massive benefits but would hand over the reins when the suits completed the takeover in two to five years. We would walk away with more money than we could imagine and become 'advisors' if we so wished. Jocelyn was very excited, but I was full of doubts.

Eventually Jocelyn persuaded me that this was a unique opportunity.

'If we don't sell he'll just copy our business model and his own team will reap the rewards. I know he'll just spit us out when he's drained the juice out of us, but the alternative is to see our business die!'

He'd just annihilate us with his power and money. Better to fall in with his plans and start another new venture at a later date.

So we signed our business over, after many hours of solicitor haggling and fine tuning.

The business ran for months as usual. Carol and I went on a long Caribbean cruise. Jocelyn took time off to do a trek around the Arctic with his wild adventure buddies, and we all returned to subtle changes in the business. The offices had been revamped and new expensive signs and carpets had been installed, and the staff had corporate uniforms to wear. It didn't feel like our business any more, and, of course, it wasn't.

Chapter 7

Jocelyn and I met up in his office to discuss our new direction in life. We tossed around ideas for a new business venture. Jocelyn was legally trained and had a finance/insurance background. I was a salesman from the world of motor vehicles. We decided to research motor vehicle warranties.

'This is your area, Jocelyn, insurance and risk,' I said.

'I disagree, old boy,' he said haughtily. 'It's more about mechanics and engineering, nuts and bolts! I will, however, talk to some pals to see if the numbers stack up.'

Less than a week later an animated Jocelyn was beaming as he put together a business plan based purely on accountancy logic.

The numbers and the projections looked very impressive. Growth patterns, profit ratios and so on. This was Jocelyn in his element. However, to me it was figures on paper, without any soul. I let myself be talked into proceeding by Jocelyn and Carol, but I was very reluctant.

I'd insisted on a feasibility study and, to make things more real, we hired an old hand in the motor extended warranty field. John Thompson had worked in the motor industry for forty-plus years. He had started in the parts department in an Austin dealership and moved into sales. When a young family came along he entered the fledgling world of motor vehicle warranties. Now, at sixty-two years of age John wanted to spend more time on the golf course. He had been senior accounts director at the largest warranty company in the UK, which underwrote all the major manufacturers' extended warranties. After a health scare and with the increased workload, John had decided to take early retirement. He was the perfect candidate to charter the tricky waters of this new venture.

At first he was not interested in any further involvement in the warranty business. However, when we explained that he could choose his hours, his role and the flexible nature of a new fledgling company he became very enthusiastic.

'If we take this ship off the ground I want to be a partner in the business,' he said, mixing his metaphors. 'I've had enough of working for big business as an employee. I want a say in the way things are run and which direction to head!'

'Aye, aye, Captain,' I replied, but he missed my attempt at humour. 'It's your baby, John – you set up a working model, tell us what you need, but please aim for the profitable side of the business at a volume that's comfortable for everyone!'

John presented a notional model of a warranty company based in our area for small-to-middle-sized independent used car dealers. Affordable products with a fair and reasonable cover for garage owner and motorist alike. He would recruit and train all staff and would have a small team of salespeople on the road to attract the business. The same sales team would vet suitable repair garages at which the technical engineers could authorise repairs. We would need two such engineers on our payroll. All others would be on an independent agency fee basis. Our office would be on small, low-overhead rental premises.

'Everything needs to be seat-of-the-pants until we turn a profit,' said John.

I could see he and I would get on. We were old-school 'don't run before you can walk' people.

'What about the figures?' asked Jocelyn.

John presented turnover, costings, projected gross and net profits, and Jocelyn's face beamed.

'Very impressive,' he said, 'but are they achievable?'

'I've erred on the side of caution and projected for calamities, so they're more than achievable,' said John, 'and just remember, if all else fails, "It's not covered, sir, because it's fair wear and tear" will become a well-worn phrase for our telesales advisors.'

We all looked at each other and realised that sentence alone would make us a lot of money.

The next decision to be made would be a name. Many warranty companies had traded over the years on trustworthy names. These projected an image of complete protection against vehicle breakdowns, regardless of whether the machine was already faulty or 'worn out' before the hapless new owner took delivery of his new toy. The best course of action would not promise total protection for a used motor vehicle. Better to be realistic and explain that only major components would be covered by our fledgling warranty company. Therefore 'autoprotect' and 'complete cover' were two phrases to avoid. We thought 'Allsop Automotive Assure' had a certain ring to it. None of the three partners was an Allsop, but 'All Seat of the Pants' summed up our virgin venture into the unknown!

The next two months were busily spent equipping our new premises with desks, phones, telephone links and office furniture bought at auction. Our original Max Value premises had a large office area to the rear of the building. With paint and carpet it soon became a cosy Allsop head office.

Although John had been an upwardly mobile executive in a suit, he now was a jack of all trades, fitting out his new offices. He relished his new role and was a dynamo of energy. Every subject I quizzed him about he'd thought of and had cost-effective answers for. From recruitment to customers he had ideas. He had a computer whizzkid to design a simple website. He had interviewed several youngsters for his telesales team and had brought Marianne from his old company to be his assistant. He'd worked out his pricing and warranty cover and had 10,000 colour leaflets printed.

Now all we had to do was promote our business. It was decided that we would concentrate on all the small-to-medium-sized garages in the South West. We could only compete on price. As we were half the price of the established warranty companies we needed to cover ground quickly. Working within the motor trade and knowing the players helped greatly, and with Robbie's help we soon signed up twelve local independent garages. A healthy start! Over the coming months and with two field reps covering the South West we slowly reached our target of a hundred garages signed up to be warranty providers.

Jocelyn had a keen young nephew straight out of university who was desperate to work, and who agreed to be our first representative on a commission-only basis. Miles was brilliant. A young engineering graduate who was very keen on all vehicles, his natural enthusiasm seemed to work on even the most cynical garage proprietor. He brought in so much business so quickly that Jocelyn suggested another contact.

Charles Summers was an old school friend of Jocelyn. He sailed close to the wind, just this side of honest. His morals were tainted more by mischief than greed. He was slightly lazy, with the attitude of 'minimum effort equals maximum reward'. However, what a salesman he was. The phrase 'Tell them what they want to hear, old boy!' was his trademark, together with his Savile Row suit, Crombie greatcoat, Jermyn Street shirts and gold cufflinks. His highly polished shoes always seemed to secure an appointment wherever he went.

Soon our sales force were upsetting our rivals. After the usual teething trouble, John had the telesales team well drilled. Daily meetings and Marianne's unflappable nature seemed to keep the sales ship on an even keel.

Our cause was greatly enhanced by a national newspaper's investigative report on the major warranty companies. Their findings were damning. The major players were accused of a cartel with the main dealers. The article suggested that customers were given a raw deal and that, far from covering the car, warranties were an expensive means of overcharging the main dealer's hapless customer for regular servicing work. The warranties were far too expensive to purchase and reduced competition because the main dealer was setting the prices. 'Highway robbery at main dealers' was the headline.

Almost immediately enquiries were being made to our telesales team. Could the callers purchase our warranty? We sent them to their nearest local non-franchise garage, who gleefully signed them up. Allsop were scoring well with our garage trade partners.

During a conversation with Jocelyn it emerged that he had 'tipped off' an old university colleague who happened to be a freelance journalist affiliated to the *Daily Herald*. Jocelyn had explained that the big warranty companies who underwrote the extended warranties for the big manufacturers and main agents were operating a 'cartel'. He had gleaned this information from John and other colleagues in the finance world. After a meeting with John and James Henry, the journalist, they had decided to delve and publish their facts and findings.

It dropped quite a bombshell amongst the big garage groups and warranty companies. So much so that the BTV television programme *Investico* decided to produce a special. This could only improve sales for Allsop and our garage customers.

The next six months produced massive growth for our company. We had to move to a large purpose-built office in Bradeley's new Riverwells Industrial Park. Extra staff were recruited and business was booming. Small garage groups joined our warranty empire, wishing to distance themselves from the pariahs reported on the *Investico* TV programme.

Carol once again highlighted a fundamental truth of our success. 'You're so busy being successful, Mark, that you've no time to enjoy it and live normally.'

She was right; life was a succession of meetings and appointments. Everything was business-related and days into weeks became a blur.

'Get Robbie, John and Jocelyn to take more of your workload and step back! You'll see the bigger picture. We don't need the money; we need time!'

Again, of course, she was right. I saw life as one big business plan with no time for hobbies or family activities.

'From now on,' said Carol, 'you tell Jocelyn that weekends are sacred because we are renovating our old cottage together.'

'What old cottage?'

But I knew as soon as I drew breath that Carol had a plan and it was pointless arguing.

'The one I've just bought at auction.' She showed me a picture of a large wreck that had seen much better days. 'It's near Bilchester in the Cotswolds and has a fabulous heritage. It's going to be our new home but needs a lot of work! So, Mark, you'd better get used to putting in a shift at weekends instead of getting flabby sitting in an office all day!'

Chapter 8

My mobile phone had never been used more than in the eight months it took to renovate that old cottage. Not that I wasn't working; I was. It was just one call after another. The most impatient message came from Jocelyn, who had been approached by a city consortium hoping to buy out Allsop. Although running Allsop had taken over Jocelyn's business life, we both knew we were happier brokering deals. His old life was more in his style.

'Tell them we'll sell only if they buy the Cotswold sites and the estate agency business. The staff and Robbie and John have to be included in any deal with guaranteed contracts.'

'Wow, an easy sell, then,' replied Jocelyn.

Two months later an agreement was made. The warranty and estate agency businesses were sold. However Robbie was keen to grow the Cotswold operations. The City acquisition Globespec were not keen to embrace a used car operation. It did not fit their corporate image.

Carol was delighted that I was now a youngish retired millionaire with hands soiled by my building labourer exploits.

Although labouring was all I could do on 'Noakes Cottage', I was busying myself with employing tradesmen who were now at the end of the rebuild. The carpets and the decorating were all that was left for the freshly plastered rooms to be completed. Of course Carol had been in her element choosing bathroom, bedroom, kitchen fittings. She had employed an interior designer who made an excellent job of creating space, light and features of all the rooms. The garden had been landscaped by a business colleague of Jocelyn, who had escaped city life for the joys of the outdoor world. 'Labour of love and a lack of pressure: what's not to love?' he said.

*

Next door to the post office in the nearby village of Bilchester was the Fighting Cocks public house, run by Mick Flanagan, a genial Irishman. He ran a typical olde worlde 400-year-old inn, all low beams, horse brasses, flagstone floors and small rooms.

'Yes, the place is haunted, alright.' His Irish burr boomed across the public bar. 'By the ghost of the debt collector. Now get yer money out and buy your round, you tight Scot.'

With this a ruddy-faced, ginger-haired stocky Glaswegian grinned, revealing several gaps where molars should have been. 'Ach, away with yer, back to yer peat bog.' The banter was just beginning.

This went on for several minutes before Mick noticed Carol and me now standing at the bar, being entertained by the floor show. Introductions were made and Carol entered into her fact-finding routine.

Mick was all too pleased to talk about himself and

family. He'd run pubs in Ireland, London and now the countryside of the Cotswolds. Married to Bridget, he had four children and two Great Danes. He'd run the Fighting Cocks for little over a year now, taking over from a family dynasty who'd let the pub slide to near closure. Now owned by Mercantile Inns, Mick had a tough lease to repay. He loved the area and the village but was struggling to boost the trade from a low start.

'I just need more time in the day to organise extra events to add a little jam on the bread,' was his colourful summary of a business plan. 'We need theme nights to unstick them bums from the easy chairs in front of the gogglebox, so we do, so we do. There's plenty of money in this area. It's just like hacking a limpet off a rock, getting it out of them.' He cast an accusing glance at Ian McDonald, our ginger Scotsman. 'Mentioning no names.'

My mind was whirring that night. Trying to sleep in our new king-size bed was proving difficult. I was so relaxed and stress-free in this new life, all I could think of was what to do next. There were only so many amazing holidays or days away and I was too young to retire and write my life story. What about Mick's pub? It would be a shame for the pub to fail. The heart of the village would be ripped out. The cabaret which was Mick would be lost. What could I do to help him? Then I had a germ of an idea. I needed to run it past Jocelyn in the morning. Hmmm.

Jocelyn at first was very sceptical. 'More scalps lost in the pub and restaurant trade than any other, old boy,' he said. 'All hard work, long hours and low margins, not to mention the fiddling amongst the staff.'

'Well, don't mention any of that, then,' I replied. 'So how come the brewery business is so massive?'

'Aah, well, it's like this,' said Jocelyn. 'You need the money up front; it's the business borrowing and the interest rate repayments that cripple the business in the first two years. Once you are past that hurdle and have built a good business it's just a question of routine and plate spinning. Most businesses that have a cashflow problem in the initial few years spiral out of control and can never repay the debt.'

'So it'd take the risk out of start-ups if we could devise a business plan to guarantee funding for a share of profit,' I said.

'It would,' said Jocelyn, 'but who would be mad enough to risk money on such a basis?' He looked at me out of the corner of his eye. 'Oh, no. No, no, no, you can't risk it, Mark. Why don't you just put your feet up or go fishing or something?'

Talking to Carol that evening, she seemed mildly interested in my musings. Of course I kept the subject low-key and concentrated on the Fighting Cocks from the angle of keeping a local community asset solvent. However, I had a plan in mind to franchise my operation across the whole of the country.

If Carol wondered during the next few weeks why we spent many days enjoying pub lunches, going out for evening meals and looking for the perfect Sunday roast, she didn't mention it. I, of course, was checking premises, prices and procedures, noting good practices, cheerful staff and management and value for money. Sadly, many establishments were badly run. Systems were chaotic and staff seemed bewildered. The simple task of serving drinks seemed beyond them. Once a substandard meal came out of the kitchen, the damage was done. No apology or discounts could rescue the situation. Prevention was certainly better than cure.

We went countrywide and soon settled on two or three favourites from the dozens of pubs that we had tried. Those three were always busy, car parks full, with a positive atmosphere, and were exciting places to be. I had noted beer, cider, spirit and wine prices, food prices and menu lists.

Talking to Mick on a quiet Tuesday morning, I crunched some numbers and calculated the margins involved. Food was obviously the main profit source. Between the two of us we calculated that, by slashing the beer prices and providing good, wholesome, plain food at low prices, we could double Mick's footfall.

'But I wouldn't want to become a busy fool,' was Mick's main concern.

I convinced him that if the Fighting Cocks developed a good name and reputation people would travel. Economies of scale would help cut his purchase prices on food and beer. His overheads would always be fixed, but he could double his income. With hard work and a positive attitude he could develop his business month on month.

'What have you got to lose, Mick? If things don't develop as planned you just revert to Plan A.'

'But I will need advertising and extra staff. Where's the money from that coming from?'

'I'll sort that,' I said. 'It won't cost you a penny!'

'But why would you do that, Mark? You don't owe me anything and I might not be able to pay you back.'

'Oh, Mick, if what I have planned works you'll pay me back a thousandfold.'

That evening I discussed my thought with Carol over supper.

'I wondered what all of those pub tours were about,' she said, laughing. 'And there's me thinking you were being romantic or you didn't like my cooking.'

'Well, that as well.' I ducked as a cushion sailed over my head, just missing the cat. 'Seriously, Mick's agreed to try a little experiment to see if we can magnify the footfall at the Cocks. When it starts, you and I may have to get our hands dirty and do some real work.'

'Hmph. Thought there would be a catch,' Carol said, but with an excitement in her voice and a twinkle in her eye. 'It'll take me back to my barmaid days when I was a student. Always being chatted up, I was, so watch out.'

What a difference between Sue and Carol, I thought. If Sue had that information she would have poured ice cold water on the idea and found every reason not to help.

*

The next two weeks were buzzing with activity. New menus were printed, and the chef was engaged to simplify everything. Luckily, Sam the Polish chef was very flexible. He was happy for Mick to run front of house. He was very grateful for the job and bought into all our aims and suggestions. Full-page adverts were taken out in the local press, and an advertisement feature was run with Mick's goals and plans for his 'new look' pub, illustrated with photographs of Mick and his staff.

The first week saw both locals and inquisitive strangers enjoying the cheaper beer and food. After some early teething problems with demand were sorted out and Carol began to help in the kitchen with Sam, exhausted smiles told us we were on the right road. Footfall and profits more than doubled in less than four months.

'I told you it was a great idea,' said Mick. 'The simple ideas are always the best. We are going to need to increase the car park size next if this continues.'

'Never mind the car park; get some more tables and chairs in here,' piped up one of the locals. 'It's standing room only some nights.'

Jocelyn read the figures from the Fighting Cocks balance sheet. He took down the relevant food and drinks figures. He crunched the overheads and staff wages into his calculations. He asked about rent, rates and advertising costs.

'Hmm,' he finally said. 'Good job you came along, Mark. I think Mick would have struggled if you hadn't changed the operation.' But Jocelyn was far from convinced. 'The amount of capital involved is eye-watering, Mark, and the cost of staff and overheads means there's little margin for complacency or quiet spells. What if they put a bypass in the village? You lose your passing trade. There are so many unforeseen—'

'What if aliens invade or all alcohol is banned?' I screeched at him before he could finish.

'Alright, old boy, touché. Just playing devil's advocate. I'm not saying on paper you haven't done a bloody good job; I'm just not totally comfortable with the amount of money needed to scale this up. Let me do some number crunching and talk to some people in the City. I'll get back to you in a few days.'

We left on a handshake.

Two weeks later an excited Jocelyn called on my mobile. 'I'm with Tristan here in Piccadilly, old boy.' He sounded tipsy. 'We'll catch the 2.30 tomorrow. Collect us from the station, there's a good chap.'

At 4.45 Jocelyn and Tristan disembarked from the first-class carriages.

'Meet Tristan, equity fund management at Schneider's, Mark. He's head of the largest cooperation specialising in the brewery and leisure industry.' I was met by a nervous-looking young city type, all expensive Savile Row suit and wet fish handshake. 'We've some ideas and figures for you.'

The next three hours were full of forecasts and projections for the future of the leisure industry in accountant speak, the gist of which was that inexpensive basic hotels and coffee shops were currently in vogue and that pubs and small hotels would see shrinkage, not growth. However, a small chain of franchised pubs in the Bradeley area could see a reasonable return on the capital invested. The accountants weighed everything in the negative, recession-induced light. I pointed out Mick's success, but fact and figures were more relevant than personalities to this pair.

Our compromised agreement was that we should find ten properties in the county that would lend themselves to a franchise model. Tristan would fund the operation through his equity partners in Schneider's, with director guarantees being provided by Jocelyn and me. Jocelyn would be the finance and purchase brain and I would locate premises and franchises. We would need to provide a franchise model loosely based upon our success in the estate agency world to satisfy Tristan's people at Schneider's.

'Just draw up figures to impress Jocelyn,' said Tristan. 'You know how to project a golden balance sheet.' He chuckled as he waved through the taxi window on his return to the railway station.

'Just got to think of a name now and then we're in the pub game,' Jocelyn intoned.

'What about "Churchill's Group", Mark?' asked Carol. 'That would impress old Caruthers from the Fighting Cocks.' She was talking about an old army bachelor who almost lived in our local hostelry, regaling anyone who would listen with stories of Korea and Aden during the years after his national service based in Libya.

'That's it,' I said.

'What, you like my suggestion of Churchill's? I was only—'

'No, no,' I replied, 'Caruthers Taverns. It's got a ring to it.' And our adventure began.

Mick's face was a picture of bewilderment, before joy and an easing of tension flooded his expression. 'Bejabbers, the Lord's answered my prayers.'

I'd explained a rough plan of how we would finance ten or so pubs in the county, freeing the owners or landlords to run the business without money trouble. It would be a cooperative franchise arrangement to improve purchasing power and advertising budgets. This was the one area that troubled Mick. He saw his role as a landlord and a host, not an accountant.

'Welcome on board, Mick,' I said. 'Just another nine to find.'

Mick gave me a list of pubs and owners he'd met through the Licensed Victuallers. Some looked interesting. One thing was for sure: Carol and I would have some fun sampling their offerings, all strictly in the name of research.

And so it proved that over the following days and weeks, together with a teasing advertisement in the *Licensed Business Weekly*, we drew up a list of potential hostelries. Some were downright awful, others were well run. Some had obvious potential. Some landlords listened to my pitch, others were totally dismissive. But most were interested to hear how they could allay their financial fears.

One by one we collected five and explained the terms of our franchise. We were completely flexible with their existing tenancy or ownership agreements. We just wanted to have a management arrangement whereby our cooperative buying powers saved them money for a small percentage of their net profit.

Jocelyn handled the bank managers' and accountants' questions and concerns as he persuaded all parties that Caruthers Taverns were taking all of the financial risks.

Soon all six pubs in our group had all-new signage, fresh advertising, special offers and uniformed staff. The image of every pub was more professional without affecting the individual premises. All the landlords were encouraged to converse with each other and help with stock, staff, training and so on. Each pub reported an increase in footfall and therefore profit due to the improved advertising.

'It's early days, Mark, but I think this may have legs,' said Jocelyn, grinning. 'Just need to roll this out to ten and then maybe the economies of scale will show a real difference. At the moment our share is losing money due to start-up costs, but the landlords are quids in.' This, of course, was always the case.

We found the other four pubs rather easily. The owners came to us when they heard through the trade grapevine of the increase in their rivals' profits. They were hungry for answers. Some pubs were too close to our existing six, others were just too small to be viable. However, four larger premises in prime locations were signed.

After four months of trading the figures were very impressive. Jocelyn and I sat down to discuss the next step. We both agreed that the model was sound. Profits were steady but not life-changing. The real aim would be to own the pubs outright. We could buy the leases or freeholds of any future premises and have tangible assets. But again, as Jocelyn said, this was a long-term undertaking with massive capital requirements. There would be refurbishment and maintenance costs and issues with finding and training good quality managers and landlords.

'Well, there must be pubs out there to buy,' I said, 'and we can experiment with one or two and see.'

'Okay, but pass it through Carol first, for goodness' sake,' said Jocelyn.

Carol was only concerned about the time commitment to another business plan. 'You don't need stress, Mark, but then again stress seems to need you,' was her cryptic summation of my plan.

With Jocelyn and Tristan's City connections, a small family-run brewery and seventeen pubs were noted to be in financial difficulties in nearby Wadwoodshire in the neighbouring Cotswold countryside.

'The Randle's Brewery chairman is Johnny Randle,' said Jocelyn. 'I went to Stoat public school with him. Never was the sharpest tool in the box. Lost all the family silver with his gambling. Hocked up to the eyeballs. His bank want a quick fire sale to minimise any embarrassment all round. Just let me negotiate, Mark. I've seen the accounts. They're into the Grosvenor bank for £4.7 mil. Business, if solvent, with the freeholds, is worth 3 million. But with any unpleasant creditors and Her Majesty's inspectors in the wings I reckon we could settle for nearer two. Just leave it to us. In the meantime here's a list of the pubs and their addresses.'

The following three weeks were spent touring the Randles' establishments across the county of Wadwoodshire. Although obviously lacking recent investment the properties were solid, if old-fashioned. The catering and image were dated thirty years in the past. Business was slow and tired. There would certainly need to be a fresh injection of capital to refresh all of the hostelries to modern standards.

One building eclipsed all the others. The Danberry Arms Hotel, although a throwback to bygone times, was in a superb setting on the edge of a beautiful Cotswold village. Set back from the green and duck pond, it belonged to another age. With work and a sympathetic makeover this could be the jewel in the crown. Carol fell in love with the whole area and, although initially sceptical about the whole undertaking, she was beginning to thaw.

Initial negotiations with the Grosvenor bank did not bode well. Their valuation of the Randle's Brewery business was near to £5 million. They wished to clear their shareholders' commitment. However, when Jocelyn reminded them of the depth of insolvency from the last set of accounts they were clearly embarrassed. Somebody at the bank had obviously taken their eye off the business. Johnny Randle had plundered any financial assets he could. He had second-charged the properties in the group and amassed massive debts. Jocelyn was in a position of strength to hardball the situation. The bank were massively exposed to an imminent collapse of the business.

'Time's on our side, Mark,' said Jocelyn. 'Just let them stew. I don't think the bank would like this can of worms to hit the press, as I've hinted will happen if they don't get real, and I can't see many other consortiums wanting to spend too much time or money on seventeen pubs which are basically stuffed.'

And so it proved to be. When the bank realised the amount of indebtedness, their vulnerable position and Randle's deviousness they negotiated hard with Jocelyn. We eventually purchased clear title to all seventeen properties and the insolvent business for £1.575 million. We set aside £2.5 million to revamp the pub chain with Tristan and Jocelyn's consortium matching my investment pound for pound as an equal and joint venture. Our grand plan was to include celebrity chef Eamon Hargreaves as our 'face' and consultant. Carol pitched in with plenty of ideas and promotions, all to be implemented within the next six months.

The pubs were rebranded as the 'Marco Mediterrano' restaurant chain to achieve a more twenty-first-century approach to Cotswold living. The publicity, menus and advertising programme were in place with internet discount vouchers to increase attendance. All the establishments had received makeovers and staff trained with the new tills and centralised uniforms, stock and ordering systems. Staff uniforms became the norm. Carol oversaw all the changes, making the Danberry Arms her headquarters.

Progress was slow but steady and soon exciting increases in profits began to emerge. We aimed at families with our new, less stuffy approach to quality dining. Eamon's persona and modern take on our venture worked perfectly and his TV catering programme went from strength to strength. Life was hectic but good.

The next two years were the happiest times Carol and I could have wished for. New friends and colleagues were found. Business was expanding, not without problems, but with a positive, can-do attitude these were solved. Every day presented new challenges that needed all of our attention. Jocelyn and I had regular meetings and agendas and generally he and Tristan's Schneider consortium seemed content.

The first clouds on the horizon came with the stock market problems. Although not directly affecting our business, the national economy and outlook were gloomy. House prices had stagnated and fallen, and money lending and finances were tight. All of the pubs in the cooperative and Caruthers Taverns noticed a reduction in trade. In the first few months with careful budgeting and belt-tightening this did not affect profits. However, as the months edged worryingly towards the busy Christmas period, the recession continued unabated. Daily news bulletins intensified the mood of depression and despair. People became scared of spending. They decided to wait for the storm to pass and stayed at home. Takings were markedly down on previous months. This was one of Jocelyn's 'told you so' moments. In all fairness to him, he never once uttered a negative thought throughout this grim period.

Christmas came and went, raising our spirits for a few weeks. However, January and February were a disaster. One of the coldest winters on record caused chaos to industry and seemed to reflect the mood of the nation. The thaw in March brought a slight respite, but March and April came and went and the groups' trading figures for the past six months were miserable.

We were not alone and high street casualties made for a nightly news gloomfest. Some of the biggest names in retail were in trouble and the banks and financial institutes were very nervous. Tristan, Jocelyn and I decided to grit our teeth and weather the storm. Although the rest of the year was very flat we managed to keep afloat.

The following year was extremely tough for the leisure and catering industry. Pubs and restaurants that were not efficient went to the wall. Tristan and Jocelyn did a splendid job of financial control and although we had slight losses during the quieter winter period we managed the business well, maintaining all our commitments and keeping our entire pub chain intact. Staff numbers were reduced slightly by natural wastage, and all but fixed costs were reduced.

We took a break in the south of Africa and for two short weeks Carol and I enjoyed the delights of this contrasting continent. Doom and gloom awaited our return and the newspaper headlines screamed that the recession was not over. However, through gritted teeth and hard work we managed to put on a brave face to our staff, motivating and cajoling one day at a time.

The City had been badly hit over this period, but we comforted ourselves with the thought that people still had to eat and drink.

Schneider's, however had no such thoughts. Spooked by a massive commodities crash in Asia, they had become very nervous and were looking at all of their UK-based commercial investors. 'Nothing to fret about, old boy,' said Jocelyn. 'They've got bigger fish to fry than us, and we are relatively stable compared to some of the big boys.'

It was just that comment about the large groups underwritten by Schneider's that proved to be ironic. The larger concerns in Schneider's business empire were too big to be allowed to fail. Due to a combination of the old school tie, the Old Pals Act and the sheer shock and panic of allowing any of these institutions to fail, the axe was poised over smaller, more solvent companies. Jocelyn was odd and distant. He was not returning my phone calls.

Eventually after almost two weeks I confronted a very sheepish, stuttering Jocelyn. He finally delivered the bombshell that Schneider's were withdrawing their support for all but the largest fish in their portfolio. Therefore Tristan was to withdraw from our business plan. Jocelyn was in a very difficult position and therefore Caruthers Taverns needed new capital investment. Between Jocelyn and me we could just about raise the capital investment to buy out Schneider's share, but it was very tight and left us very exposed. 'Don't worry, old boy,' said Jocelyn, 'I'll put out feelers with my City chums and contacts.'

Three weeks elapsed and Jocelyn's efforts proved fruitless. 'I'm about as popular as a turd in a swimming pool,' he said, in an effort to lift the gloom. 'Schneider's are pressing for the buyout proposal we haven't got, or they'll sell their share to the highest bidder or just foreclose.'

'Offer them half of what they want, Jocelyn. We'll wing it to get the best deal but we can't rely on anyone else. It's very cold out there when you're exposed,' I said.

We eventually reached an agreement with Schneider's after many meetings in their Victorian boardroom. They realised that they were in a weak position, but they still had enough power to pull the rug from under us. They took the view that their shareholders needed to be 'risk averse'. Jocelyn and I were lectured like schoolboys; we were made to feel we were the devil's apprentices incarnate and had wronged Schneider's because we dared to oppose them and not to pay what they wanted. Our solicitors quickly drew up the paperwork and soon Caruthers Taverns were wholly owned by me and Jocelyn. The split was 75:25, purely because I had the greater purse, and this reflected my ingoings, not my professional opinion of Jocelyn.

The next six months were very tough. As Jocelyn had warned, cashflow and the amount of capital required stretched everything. Without Schneider's unlimited funds we had to juggle like a Russian circus. Our Midshires bank restricted us to choking point and pleas for help fell on deaf ears. The bank's umbrella for a rainy day was well and truly in the closet, not to be used. The government didn't help with their choking financial policies, and in March the bombshell of the smoking ban was announced. No wonder I was taking to drinking myself to sleep with a daily ration of half a bottle of scotch before bedtime.

Gloom followed bad results followed more pressure, resulting in sleepless nights or hungover mornings. There seemed to be no end. Jocelyn tried to raise my spirits, so too Carol. I just retreated into myself and on one particular awful day took the phones off the hook and went to bed at 6pm. I pulled the duvet over my head and stayed there for three days and nights. Carol drove me to the doctor's, but he could only offer antidepressants, not solutions to my problems. My only antidepressant came in a bottle of Highland Malt.

After one particularly bad day, shaking, I drove towards Redwell's Bridge, swerving at the last minute. I couldn't do it, so I took to the Wheatsheaf in Bridgechester; no one knew me here, or so I thought. So, three hours and ten double whiskies later, I drove home. The white police car behind me came closer, so I dodged down side streets and dark lanes; still it followed until the road came to a dead end.

'Mark, is that you?'

I've never been so pleased to hear Robbie's voice in my life. I was a quivering, drunken mess. He helped me into his car and somehow drove me to his house.

Next morning I felt absolutely terrible in every way. Every emotion from embarrassment to disgust with myself, to stubborn stupidity. I was in denial and needed to talk. Hours later Robbie took me to collect my car, not before we had some soul-searching, talking and a plan for recovery. Robbie had phoned Carol and now they were talking together in hushed tones. I felt stupid and ashamed. But I promised them both, no more drink. I was lucky not to be in jail.

I'd like to report that events improved in the next few months, but they didn't. Business was awful, Carol and I hardly spoke and I withdrew into myself. I had taken to long country walks with Samson, my faithful border collie. I retreated into a dreamlike state, overtaken by worries and demons in my head. My hands were shaking. I needed a drink.

Carol had hidden every drop of alcohol in the house except some rancid cooking sherry. I uncorked the bottle and downed the contents in three massive slugs. A warm glow engulfed my whole being. I staggered up the stairs on all fours, threw my clothes on the floor and retreated into the spare room to sleep it off.

When I woke the next day the house seemed incredibly quiet and still. 'Carol!' I shouted several times. Nothing, Samson bounded up and licked my face. 'Where's your mum?' I asked. Nothing.

Her car was missing from its spot. An uneasy feeling made me look in her wardrobe. All of her clothes were missing. I tore through the whole house; not one scrap of her was to be found. I had never felt so alone or more helpless or more hopeless. Sheer misery engulfed my soul.

Over the next few months I vowed to work myself into an early grave. I also vowed to find Carol and win her back. She had disappeared and did a wonderful job of eluding me. Her friends would not return my calls. She left town. All I could do was concentrate on the business. Jocelyn and I vowed to weather this and any other storm.

I had not touched alcohol or had a break for nearly six months when Mary, Carol's oldest friend, called me to say Carol wanted to talk.

Walking up the drive to our house, I was filled with trepidation. Carol's car was by its old spot and I noticed a suntanned Carol through the window. She looked well, if a little aloof. She told me she had been on a long journey through Asia and the Far East to meditate and reflect on life. Then she threw a bombshell. If we were to have any future, we had to change our philosophy completely. She explained how the poorest people she had encountered on her journey were amongst the happiest. She saw our westernised, materialistic life as being poisonous.

'Mark, you need to abandon your lifestyle, abandon your business life and change completely before your mental health and physical health kills you. Unless you completely change, we have no future and your life will be an empty shell.'

The words pounded in my brain and I knew immediately that she was right. 'Go on,' I said.

For the next two hours she explained her thoughts of how we were chasing an impossible dream that would ultimately result in misery. We were existing for our own selfish needs when a better, simpler life beckoned which was more rewarding to the soul.

'What do you want to do?' I asked, quivering.

'Sell up and set up a charitable organisation in Vietnam. Help orphaned kids and community coffee growers and give something back,' she stated. Carol had a steely determination and a resolve which I knew was serious.

'Okay,' was my only comment.

She looked incredulous and then a massive smile beamed across her face, followed by the biggest bear hug. A feeling of joy and peace engulfed my body.

The brewery-and-restaurant business of Caruthers Taverns was sold to a venture capitalist contact of Jocelyn's. If truth be told, even if Jocelyn thought I was mad he seemed relieved to exit the pub business. All ties with the car business were transferred to Robbie.

'But your share is worth thousands,' he said. 'How can I pay you back?'

'Just be my friend and support my new life, Robbie,' I said.

We kept our house for a base in this country. The proceeds of our business sale amounted to a little over £227,000, which would set up our new life in Vietnam, with a school, a small coffee plantation and a truck, and a village full of smiling Vietnamese as our new family.

Lightning Source UK Ltd.
Milton Keynes UK
UKOW04f2259290817
308194UK00001B/12/P